Praise for *Texas Thunder*

"Fast-paced and smoothly plotted, Raye's lighthearted series starter deftly evokes a variety of emotions while building multifaceted characters."

—*Publishers Weekly*

"A sweet, passionate story that captures the heart and provides a thrilling happily-ever-after."

—*Night Owl Reviews*

"Love and moonshine blend well in Raye's latest novel set in Texas, with her modern, amusing storytelling and strong, lively characters. Callie's sassiness is the perfect complement to Brett's toughness, and their tension is just as fiery and intense as their chemistry, which will appeal to readers. Raye gives us a well-crafted, down-home romance."   —*RT Book Reviews*

"A sizzling tale that features some hot sex, but it's the plentiful laugh-out-loud scenes that will pull readers in. A passionate and enjoyable read from beginning to end."   —*Romance Reviews Today*

Also by Kimberly Raye

Texas Thunder
Red-Hot Texas Nights

TEMPTING TEXAS

KIMBERLY RAYE

St. Martin's Paperbacks

This is a work of fiction. All of the characters, organizations, and events portrayed in this novel are either products of the author's imagination or are used fictitiously.

TEMPTING TEXAS

Copyright © 2016 by Kimberly Raye.

For information address St. Martin's Press, 175 Fifth Avenue, New York, NY 10010.

ISBN: 978-1-250-06397-7

Our books may be purchased in bulk for promotional, educational, or business use. Please contact your local bookseller or the Macmillan Corporate and Premium Sales Department at 1-800-221-7945, ext. 5442, or by e-mail at MacmillanSpecialMarkets@macmillan.com.

Printed in the United States of America

St. Martin's Paperbacks edition / November 2016

St. Martin's Paperbacks are published by St. Martin's Press, 175 Fifth Avenue, New York, NY 10010.

10 9 8 7 6 5 4 3 2 1

CHAPTER 1

"Are you sure you want to do this?"

"I've never been more sure of anything in my entire life." Except when she'd traded her Easy-Bake Oven for Donna Martin's Let's Play Veterinarian! set back when she'd been six. And when she'd rescued her now beloved Jezebel from that kill shelter a few years ago. And when she'd turned down Marty Bezdeck's marriage proposal—not once, but four times.

But this . . .

Jenna Evelyn Tucker glanced at the THREE LITTLE HIGGS CONSTRUCTION sign planted near the roadside mailbox and stiffened against the sudden fluttering in her stomach.

It wasn't like she was selling the place.

She was just overhauling. Cleaning house. Tearing down the ancient two-story eyesore and most every other building on the property and putting something new and respectable in its place.

It was the smart thing to do. The most logical given the circumstances—namely that she was all alone at the run-down property since both of her sisters had fallen head over heels in love and moved out with their significant others. The old Tucker farmhouse was too big for one person. Too worn-out for a single woman to fix up all by her lonesome. Too notorious given that her granddaddy had blown himself and his moonshine still to smithereens just beyond the edge of the tree line. The explosion had happened over a year ago, but people were still talking about it.

Still laying bets on which Tucker would set up shop and follow in his footsteps.

Certainly not the eldest. Callie was too straitlaced to ever do such a thing. And Brandy? While the middle Tucker had, indeed, come up with her very own moonshine recipe a little over six months ago, she wasn't in the backyard filling up jars and peddling them out of the back of her Buick. Rather, she'd taken a much more reputable route by selling her recipe to a cutting-edge distiller. She was now busy making cakes and pies for her bakery while raking in a decent royalty from Foggy Bottom Distillers.

No, Jenna herself was the likely choice. She'd always been ballsy and bold just like her grandfather. The first to speak her mind if the notion struck and go her own way, the world be damned. Why, no one would be surprised if she thumbed her nose at the law and started brewing her own hooch in this very backyard.

All the more reason to prove them wrong. If she wanted to change her image, to clean it up, she needed to start changing everyone's perception of her.

No more flipping off the local gossips and doing her own thing. It was time to stand up. Grow up.

Think.

Which explained why her eldest sister was staring

at her with nothing short of full-blown confusion. Jenna had never been known for using her head first and her heart second.

She let her emotions drive her, be it anger, happiness, desire, excitement, guilt. Jenna was all about feelings—the good, the bad, and the ugly.

No more.

She was going through with a major renovation, from demolition to rebuild. Until the Tucker spread looked nothing like the cover for her grandfather's illegal moonshine activities, and everything like a working horse ranch.

That's what this was all about. Erasing the past and building a brand new future. A life as a reputable vet and horse trainer.

While she'd seen herself following a different path as Rebel's number-one veterinarian, she'd hit a roadblock recently and now was the time to backtrack and blaze another trail. Her promotion at the animal clinic had fallen through, and all because of her last name.

Her reputation.

She swallowed against a sudden lump in her throat and eyed her older sister.

Callie Tucker Sawyer had the signature blond hair and green eyes of most every other Tucker, Jenna included. But unlike her youngest sister, Callie had more curves where it counted. She wasn't quite as voluptuous as their middle sister, Brandy, but close enough that she'd snagged the attention of her archenemy, Brett Sawyer, and married him much to the dismay of an entire town.

Not that Callie cared what everyone thought now the way she had when she'd been young.

She and Brett were still in the honeymoon phase of their relationship, having only been married a few months, but theirs was a love story that had been going strong since they were teenagers. A love that had drawn them together despite time away and a decades-long feud between their families that had tried to rip them apart.

"You look happy," Jenna heard herself say and Callie's frown eased into a smile.

"I am." Her eyebrows drew together again. "But you're not." The smile eased back into worry. "What's going on, Jenna? I can see you wanting to fix the place up a little, but this is way over the top. They're going to tear down the house and build from the ground up. While I'm not overly sentimental when it comes to this place—I scrubbed too many floors and cooked too many dinners to get weepy over shaking things up, but you're different. This is your home."

"You and Brandy were my home, but you're both gone now and that's a good thing." She smiled even though she didn't quite feel it. "It's time for me to do something for myself. I need a change, Callie." A big one if she wanted to alter an entire town's perception and stop living in the shadow of her legacy. She'd had her fill of the gossip. Of being wild and rambunctious and spontaneous.

And unreliable.

That's what Dr. Morris Holiday of the Rebel Veterinary Clinic had told her last week right before he'd dropped a semi across her career path, passed her over for a full-time position, and hired a first-year vet from another county with zero experience.

Jenna had been his intern for nearly two years. Two freakin' *years*. She'd worked overtime and weekends and loved every one of their patients as if they'd been her own beloved pets.

And while he recognized her hard work, he'd told her flat-out that it just wasn't enough. He wanted someone who was steady. Rock-solid. And not a Tucker.

Because Tuckers, at least according to the Sawyers, were not to be trusted, and while Dr. Morris wasn't a Sawyer himself, he had a lot of patients who were, particularly his biggest account—the Sawyer Bend Horse Farm.

No way would Thaddeus T. Sawyer let Jenna set foot on his precious three hundred acre spread, and so Dr. Morris had hired someone who could.

The truth still sat heavy in her stomach.

She'd wanted nothing more than to drive out and tell old Thaddeus exactly where to go and how to get there, but then that was exactly what he would have expected from her. From any lowly Tucker.

Because the Tuckers were volatile. No good. Trashy.

An opinion held for nearly one hundred years since Archibald Tucker had had the mother of all falling-outs with his best buddy, Elijah Sawyer. They'd been friends, business partners, and the masterminds behind the hottest-selling moonshine back in the day.

But then they'd had a vicious brawl in front of family and friends and several lawmen who'd been powerless to stop the inevitable.

The two men had beat each other to a pulp smack-dab in the middle of the town square before going their separate ways, both intent on making a go in the moonshine business on their own. And while each had cooked up some halfway decent bootleg during the Prohibition era, none of it had ever compared to the ever-popular Texas Thunder that had made the two men famous at the height of their friendship.

A recipe that had been severed all those years ago after their bloody knock-down, drag-out fight.

The town had been divided, as well, as the Sawyers sided with their kin and the Tuckers sided with theirs.

It had stayed that way over the years as the descendants of the two men had kept up the fighting and the animosity, and given Texas its own bloody version of the Hatfields and the McCoys.

Things had calmed down in recent years. No one actually shot anyone since Junior Sawyer had blown the big toe off Billy Tucker's right foot a few years back at the annual Fourth of July picnic. But the Sawyers still hated the Tuckers, and the Tuckers still gave them tit for tat.

Except for Callie and Brandy. They'd both married Sawyers—Callie's modest wedding had been a few months back and Brandy's elopement just four short weeks ago—and were as happy as ever, which meant that anything was possible.

Jenna held tight to the hope that whispered through her. She knew she couldn't change old Thaddeus's mind, so she'd decided to give him a run for his money. He bred the best horses in the county, but not for long. Jenna Tucker was setting up shop and she was going to whip his proverbial butt in the equine business.

While she couldn't change her bloodline, she could change her life. She was through feeding into the negative stereotypes that had defined the Tuckers for so long. No more running her mouth whenever the mood struck. No more dancing her ass off down at the local bar every Saturday night. And no more jumping from one guy to the next.

She'd smartened up and sworn off bad boys a few years back after a string of split-second relationships that had ended with Mr. Tall, Dark, and Bad-to-the-bone riding off into the sunset, often with another woman. Or two. And there was even that one time when Ronnie Darlington had left town with the Parker triplets, each of whom he'd dumped a few weeks later because hey, he was a rolling stone. A rodeo cowboy who couldn't be tamed. A bull-riding bad ass who had caught her eye down at the local honky-tonk.

Ronnie had opened her eyes to her addiction and forced her to go cold turkey. No more hot, wild, disreputable men who were terrible at relationships but great in bed.

And so she'd moved on to not-so-hot, tame, reputable men who'd been great at relationships, but terrible in bed. Men who'd been devoted and faithful and so boring that she'd been the one to bail each and every time.

In a nice way, of course. So nice, in fact, that several on her long list of good guys had failed to take the hint. She was still getting flowers from a few of them. And open declarations of love. And there was even that marriage proposal a few months back.

Just the thought of spending the rest of her life with a man who loved *The Bachelor* as much as she did was enough to scare some sense into her. She was through with any and all relationships for now.

She was toning things down, rising above her name, and walking the straight and narrow all by her lonesome.

Step one—she needed to change her surroundings. She and her sisters had been living hand to mouth since their parents had died over ten years ago. But in the past year, things had turned around.

Callie and Brett had found the original Texas Thunder recipe and decided to sell it to a local distillery. Callie had generously split her share of the profits with Brandy and Jenna. Meanwhile Brandy had refined the original into something all her own and was now banking royalties from every batch sold of her popular Texas Tornado. With both of her sisters holding their own financially, they'd seen no need to hold onto the Tucker spread. They'd signed over their shares to Jenna and now she was the sole owner.

She'd taken out a homeowner's loan for the renovations just last week and signed the paperwork with Brody Higgs from Three Little Higgs early that morning.

She shoved the construction sign into the dirt and drew a deep breath. Her gaze swept the horizon. The sun had started to set and orange edged the rich green that marked the height of spring in Texas.

Her attention shifted to the house and the shadows creeping in from the east. The paint was peeling, the porch sagging. The bottom step near the door had given way beneath her boot just yesterday and now sat cracked and splintered. The place was an eyesore, despite the warm light that gleamed in the windows and the smell of apples that drifted from the kitchen courtesy of a couple of Brandy's famous turnovers warming in the oven.

Something tugged inside of her and she focused on the rain gutter that hung off the left corner. There weren't enough turnovers to make her ignore the sad state of the place. She'd done that far too long already.

"The bulldozer arrives tomorrow," she told Callie, dusting her hands off on her cutoff shorts, "which means I'd better get busy." She started toward the house. "They're going to start with the barn first, but that will go down within the week. I need to get everything out of the house in the meantime."

"I can help," Callie called after her. "I've already turned in my column at the newspaper. I could call Brett and let him know I'll be late."

"Thanks, sis, but you've cleaned this place long enough." Jenna shook her head and didn't let her steps waver. "It's my turn."

CHAPTER 2

Hunter DeMassi was about to get his ass blown to hell and back.

The truth coiled his muscles tight. Anxiety knotted his stomach and cranked the vise in his chest. He forced a deep breath. Rather than ease the tautness in his body, the extra burst of oxygen fed his worry.

It didn't matter that he had a Glock strapped to his hip and a badge stuffed into his left pocket. If anything, those two items painted him as an even bigger target. It was one thing to fire a load of buckshot into some unknown sonofabitch who happened to be in the wrong place at the wrong time, and quite another to take out the one man intent on shutting down the biggest moonshine operation in the entire Lone Star state.

A setup not more than fifty yards away from where he crouched behind a massive oak tree. It was early evening, the sky overhead dotted with stars, but none of that light made its way down through the dense foliage.

He squinted, his eyes quickly adjusting to the darkness and the small clearing littered with debris. An old washing machine. An ancient tiller. A dingy John Deere missing all four wheels. A rusted-out shell of an ancient

'59 Ford pickup truck. His gaze zeroed in on the spiral of smoke whispering from the tailpipe. The scent of warm yeast filled the air and the hair prickled on the back of Hunter's neck.

These guys were smart.

His gaze scoured the rest of the area, from what looked like a haphazard line of tin cans scattered near the tree line at the edge of the clearing.

Smart and a little bit old school.

Which made whoever was responsible for the setup even more deadly.

The old-timers came from a different era where the only law involved a Remington and a box of shells. A man did what he had to do to protect his livelihood. His life. Whether he was up against a stranger, or someone wearing a badge. The details made no nevermind.

It was all about survival.

Hunter had learned that a long, long time ago, on the knee of his great-grandmother who'd told him all about the old days and her daddy's infamous Texas Thunder.

Not that Elijah Sawyer had been the one solely responsible for the state's most notorious moonshine. He'd had a partner back then, a man by the name of Archibald Tucker. He and Archibald had been as close as brothers. But then they'd had a falling-out, ripped their precious recipe right down the middle so neither could keep brewing the popular stuff, and parted ways. Their fight had caused a riff that had run deep and divided the entire town. But Elijah hadn't wasted any time crying over the loss of his best friend or his meal ticket. He'd taken all the cash he'd stashed when Texas Thunder had been selling like hotcakes and gone the straight and narrow.

Which had been his plan all along.

While Archibald Tucker had fit the old moonshine mentality to a tee—he'd liked drinking just as much as he'd liked brewing—Elijah Sawyer had been looking at the stuff from a monetary standpoint. A means to an end. Legend had it that he'd never even touched a drop of the brew other than to taste for quality control. Instead, he'd kept his head clear and his mind focused. He'd wanted more than a few coins in his pocket and a Mason jar in his hand—he'd wanted to make something of himself, his family, and he'd done just that. He'd bought up the land around Rebel, Texas and turned it into one of the biggest cattle ranches in the South.

"You can make it, too," his great-grandmother had told him time and time again. When he'd been eight years old and barely passing because a bad case of dyslexia had made school nearly impossible. When he'd called it quits his junior year at Rebel High to work at the local rodeo arena and help bust broncs. When he'd left town to travel the circuit because his choices had been too few and far between, and living on the edge had paid the most money.

He hadn't listened to her. Not until he'd come home six years later for his youngest brother's funeral. A brother who'd stayed the course, graduated at the top of his class, gone off to college, and then straight into the Marines. Travis had never run from anything difficult. He'd worked hard to make their parents proud. To make something of himself. To live up to the prestigious Sawyer name.

"It isn't too late to step up and do the right thing," Mimi had told him as she'd sat next to him in that first

church pew, the smell of gardenias from the casket spray nearly suffocating him. *"You can do this, Hunter. You can turn it around and be a steady hand just like Travis."*

She'd been right.

Hunter had traded in his living-on-the-edge mentality and wandering ways, and now he was here, about to run for his third term as sheriff of Rebel County. People had been skeptical at first and he'd barely won the first race, but thanks to his Mimi and the fact that he'd been running against a low-life Tucker, folks had seen him as the lesser of two evils and given him a chance. Number two had been a landslide, and three was sure to be the same, especially since his opponent was none other than Cade Tucker. While Cade was one of the few Tuckers to rise up and amass a small fortune for himself, most of the local businesses had Sawyer roots. The Sawyers were the money behind Rebel. They always had been, and to hear his Mimi tell it, they always would be.

Even against Cade, Hunter would most certainly win.

If he could shut down the moonshine ring that was still operating in his county. That would easily top Cade's one and only claim to fame—blowing the whistle on two local nail salons that had been fronting football pots.

This was much bigger and sure to trump Naughty Nails and their little side business. That's why Hunter was out here risking his neck. No way did he like the sliver of apprehension that whispered up his spine, or the rush of adrenaline that pumped through his veins and coiled his muscles tight.

This was just part of the job.

One that he would soon hand over to the suits out of

Austin. The FBI had been breathing down his neck about this case, thirsty for details, hungry for a major collar. Which he would gladly give them. Once he had more information. Hard-core evidence.

It was all about being thorough.

No way was he out here after hours because this was the most interesting case to come across his desk since he'd discovered Buddy Roy selling marijuana brownies out of the trunk of his Kia. Sure, Hunter dealt with the occasional moonshiners, but most were local and harmless. They posed more of a threat to themselves than they did to the good citizens of Rebel.

But these guys . . . They were different. They might well be local, but they were smart, too. Cunning. And judging from the covert setup, they were most certainly moving more than a few jars of moonshine down at the VFW Hall. These shiners were going to great lengths to cover their tracks and protect their investment, which told him it was a hefty investment, indeed. That, and he just had a feeling.

That tingle that told him there was something big going on. Something dangerous. *Exciting.*

The thought struck and he pushed it away. He wasn't looking for excitement. This was all about keeping the peace in his town. Being reliable. Dependable.

He wouldn't disappoint.

Those days were long gone, buried six feet under with his little brother who'd always gone above and beyond the call of duty.

Yep, he would gather as much information as possible and then he would hand it over to the Feds. Then he would get himself over to the courthouse and file the paperwork to run for another term.

But first . . .

He eyed the small red dot blinking on a nearby tree. His gaze focused, taking in the edges and curves of the game camera attached to the sturdy wood. Another quick glance at the rest of the area and he noted another camera. And another.

Yep, these shiners were smart, all right.

So smart that he wouldn't doubt that the cameras not only took pictures, but also sent live feed to someone on the other end. Watching for trespassers. Waiting.

He moved ever so slightly and the light on the nearest tree blinked. The faintest hint of flash lit up the area and sent Hunter ducking behind the tree.

Too smart and so it was time to back off.

For now.

Hunter locked in the location on the GPS on his phone and turned. He made it several steps, picking his way slowly past the trees, moving this way and that, backtracking the way he had come. He'd almost made it, too, but then he heard the voices in the distance.

"He was right here, I tell ya. Right *here.*"

Leaves crunched, branches rustled, and just like that, he had two shiners hot on his tail.

He reached for the walkie-talkie in his back pocket. "This is Sheriff DeMassi. I need backup." He breathed a quick location before cutting his dispatcher off in midresponse and hitting the Silence button.

Stuffing the walkie-talkie back into his pocket, he picked up his steps and hauled ass.

CHAPTER 3

Jenna hauled the box down off the back porch and headed for the burn pile set up several yards away. The sun had already set and the only light came from the orange flames now licking at the star-dusted sky.

She settled the container near the pile and reached for the first of a mountain of old *Reader's Digest*s.

Her grandfather had never been one to part with anything, be it a nearly empty tube of Bengay or six large boxes full of faded magazines.

She tossed the first few issues into the fire. A spray of red embers spit back at her and she inched a few inches backward before tossing in another handful. The flames gobbled up the faded pages, sending a burst of smoke spiraling into the air.

A smile touched her lips as her gaze snagged on a cover that featured Ronald Reagan. James Harlin Tucker had never had a ready supply when it came to words of wisdom for his three granddaughters. He'd been an alcoholic barely able to take care of himself, much less the three young girls left behind when his son and daughter-in-law had died in a car accident. It had been Callie who'd been both mother and father to Brandy and

Jenna when their parents had passed on. She'd doled out all the good advice in the family. The only words James Harlin had ever passed on were the occasional *"If you want to make a really good moonshine, you have to add just a hint more honey,"* or *"George Jones might be a pretty good SOB, but he ain't got nothin' on Hank,"* or *"If we want to get this country back on track, we need another one like Ronald Reagan."*

Yep, he'd been as much a Reagan fan as he'd been into Hank Williams and hard cider shine. She curled the small magazine and shoved it into her back pocket before feeding another stack into the flames.

Not because she was a fan herself, or the least bit sentimental when it came to her grandfather. He'd been a selfish man for the most part, too intent on making his moonshine to spare any time for his granddaughters. But there had been those rare moments when he'd recited some joke from his beloved *Reader's Digest* and actually coaxed a smile out of Jenna.

Brandy and Callie, not so much. They'd been older and had never found anything remotely funny about James Harlin. But Jenna had been younger, and so it had been easier for her to look past his faults and focus on the one redeeming quality about her grandfather—he could always make her laugh.

"Only because you have the same warped sense of humor," Callie had told her too many times to count.

The same sense of humor.

The same green eyes.

The same I-don't-give-a-shit attitude.

Yep, she was definitely a chip off the old Tucker block.

Which was her main problem in a nutshell.

She forced her fingers to move, fished the magazine out of her back pocket, and tossed it onto the fire. The flames breathed a fiery sigh across the cover, the edges blackened and curled. Just like that, Ronald Reagan turned to a thick gray wisp of nothing. The smoke burned her nostrils and her chest tightened. She stiffened and forced a deep breath.

The next two hours were spent hauling out the last few boxes from James Harlin's old room, namely more *Reader's Digest*s, some old clothes that the church had turned down when they'd stopped to pick up donations, and a mountain of old receipts for all of James's sugar and corn purchases that had been hiding in the back of his closet. He could barely remember his last name at times, but he'd kept pristine track of his shine.

"We're going to make it big again," he'd always told the girls while he'd searched for the original Texas Thunder recipe. *"Bigger than back in the day. You mark my words."*

But the only thing he'd made had been a gross miscalculation that had caused an explosion that had destroyed his handmade still and everything within a twenty-yard radius. James Harlin included.

Jenna herself had been sleeping at the time. The boom had brought her fast awake, but when she and her sisters had made it out to the edge of the woods, the fire had been too widespread. They'd called 911 and watched helplessly as James and his still had gone up into a cloud of smoke along with the surrounding oak and cedar trees.

Her gaze went to what had once been a thick tree line.

The spot had been leveled, the ground now bare until it reached the new tree line farther away. The branches quivered despite the lack of a breeze. Awareness whispered over her skin and she had the sudden feeling that she wasn't alone.

Her ears perked and she listened, but only the buzz of crickets filled the night air.

Crazy.

Now that her sisters had moved out, the solitude was getting to her.

She focused on retrieving the last of the boxes Callie had packed up last year. While her sister had finally found the guts to put away their grandfather's stuff, she hadn't managed to do any more than stack the boxes. They had sat in the room, waiting for someone else to find the courage to finish what Callie had started. Brandy had stepped up to the plate next, moving everything out onto the porch and calling the church.

Only the First Presbyterian Church of Rebel hadn't been too excited over a useless pile of outdated *Reader's Digest*s and so the magazines had been left behind and tossed back into the room, waiting for someone else— namely Jenna—to step up and finish the job. And since there was no trash pick-up so far out of the city limits, she was left feeding a burn pile.

She blinked against the sudden burning behind her eyes and reached for the last box. She hauled it through the house and pulled open the back door. She was just about to shove it onto the porch when a large, dark shadow filled her line of vision and a deep, familiar voice echoed in her ears.

"Get back in the house. Now."

"Sheriff DeMassi?" she started, but before she could ask him what he was doing here, he gripped her arm, steered her around, and pushed her back inside.

"Wait a sec—" she started as he followed her in and slammed the door. The lock clicked as the one and only dead bolt on the decrepit door slid into place.

"If you want to find yourself staring down the barrel of a Beretta, keep talking." He flipped off the lights near the back, plunging the kitchen into darkness and turned to peer past the edge of the curtains. "If not, then get the rest of those lights." He motioned to the bulb gleaming in the hallway.

Jenna opened her mouth, but something about the stiff set to his broad shoulders stalled the words in her throat. She stiffened, turned on her heel, and flipped a nearby switch. Darkness descended, filling the hallway. The only other light that still burned was a lamp on James Harlin's old nightstand. A few seconds later, she'd killed the switch on it and stopped off to make sure the front door was locked before finding her way back to the kitchen. The burn pile still blazed outside, edging the kitchen curtains in a pale orange glow.

"What's going on?" she whispered after a few silent minutes of staring at his shadowy form standing sentry at the back window. Her heart echoed in her ears and her breaths came quick and shallow. "Sheriff?" she whispered again when he didn't say anything.

Rather he simply stood there, waiting, listening.

Her ears perked and that's when she heard it. The faint thud of footsteps. The crunch of grass. The cock of a trigger . . .

Just as the thought registered, the sheriff grabbed her hand, hauled her down to the floor and shielded her body with his. A shot echoed, wood cracked, and the first bullet bit through the door and whizzed overhead.

CHAPTER 4

No fucking way.

The words registered a split second before Jenna realized they weren't just in her head. Instead, the sheriff's voice echoed in her ear, his body pressing her down flat on the floor, hard muscle shielding every dip and curve and . . .

Wait a second.

No way should she be thinking about his muscles and her curves and . . . Seriously, someone had just *shot* at them.

"He's in there," came the frantic voice from outside. "He has to be in there. There's no place else to run . . ." The words faded into the blare of a siren in the distance. "*Shit.* Someone called the cops."

"That was the cops, I'm telling you. It was the sheriff. I saw him plain as day."

"That don't make a lick of sense. You can't see a blasted thing plain as day when it's full-blown night."

"I've got good vision."

"All's you saw was the back of his head."

"Yeah, well it looked like the back of the sheriff's

head and that there siren's proof that it was. He ran back to his squad car and now he's coming for us."

"Or maybe somebody just called the police because they heard the first round of gunshots a ways back. I told you not to fire."

"Think what you want. Either way, we need to get while the gettin's good."

"That's the first sensible thing you've said all night. We still got work to do." Footsteps clomped across the back porch and then grew fainter as the two men hit the ground running.

"Wait," the sheriff murmured in her ear when she started to get up.

"But they're gone."

"Maybe, and maybe not. Just give it a second. Just to be sure."

But it took more than a few seconds for Hunter De-Massi to climb off of her. It was exactly sixty-eight seconds during which Jenna did her damnedest to focus on the echo of her own heartbeat rather than the steady drum of his as he pressed her down.

The rich, intoxicating aroma of clean soap and strong male filled her head and skimmed her senses and she trembled.

"It's okay," he murmured, his grip on her tightening as if he mistook the response for fear.

Ah, but it was fear. Of the carnal variety because this was the closest Jenna had been to a member of the opposite sex since she'd sworn off men over three months ago.

Not that three months was a long time. Not for the average female, but Jenna liked men. She enjoyed them.

Or she had before she'd sworn off bad boys and given the not-so-bad boys a chance. The sex hadn't been nearly as satisfying and so, technically, her dry spell had been going on a lot longer than three months.

Try two years.

Twenty-four long, lonely months since she'd had really good sex. Long enough to make any woman a little desperate.

And stupid.

His warm breath brushed the back of her neck and her nipples pebbled in response. A shiver worked its way up her spine. Her thighs clenched.

Even though Hunter DeMassi with his do-right attitude and his conservative looks was far from the thigh-clenching type.

She reminded herself of that all-important fact when he finally pulled her to her feet. A sliver of orange slid past the edge of the drapes that covered a nearby window and sliced across his face, illuminating his features. She found herself staring up into eyes as intoxicating as a shot of her granddad's favorite blueberry moonshine, and even more potent.

Her stomach hollowed out and her throat tightened.

Hello? It's Sheriff Hunter DeMassi aka Dudley Do-Right. He walks the straight and narrow. Hell, he *is* the straight and narrow.

Which meant she shouldn't be reacting to him at all.

She knew that. At the same time, she couldn't help but notice the five o'clock shadow covering his jaw and the all-important fact that he wasn't wearing his uniform. Instead of the blah-blah beige, a soft white cotton T-shirt clung to broad shoulders and heavily muscled arms. A small rip a few inches below his collar gave her a glimpse of dark, silky hair. Faded jeans cupped his crotch and outlined his long legs. Scuffed cowboy boots completed the look and for a split second she forgot this was the same man who sat in the second row at church every Sunday and directed traffic at the senior ladies' bake sale every other Tuesday.

He looked almost . . . dangerous.

Heat whispered up her spine and she stiffened.

Dark brows drew together as he eyed her. "You okay?"

"I . . ." She swallowed against the sudden lump in her throat and forced herself to take a deep breath. "What just happened?"

"I was tracking some suspects and got a little too close. They spotted me and, well, you know the rest."

"What kind of suspects?"

He eyed her as if deciding just how much to say. "Some bad-ass mothers judging by the look of your door." He turned then, his long, tanned fingers going to the bullet hole surrounded by splintered wood. "Looks like a three fifty-seven. Maybe a Glock or a Smith and Wesson." He turned back to her then, a strange light in his eyes. "I didn't mean to put you at risk by barging in here, but I needed some cover."

"Better the door than you."

He grinned then, a slash of white that split the shadows of the room and her breath caught.

Stupid, she reminded herself. Really, *really* stupid.

"I'd better get some of these lights turned on." She gave herself a mental shake and turned as he reached for the walkie-talkie stuffed into his back pocket. Static echoed through the room a split second before Hunter started talking in a low monotone that kept her from making out more than a few words.

"A squad car picked up both suspects," he told her. "Again, I'm really sorry about the door. I'll get my deputy out here to fix it first thing tomorrow morning."

"Don't bother. That door was worn down near the hinges anyway. I'm sure it'll be the first thing to go when the renovation starts. In the meantime, I'll just stick some duct tape over the hole and she's good to go."

He arched an eyebrow. "You fixing the place up?"

"I'm *changing* the place up." She glanced around at the dingy avocado wallpaper and old-fashioned copper Jell-O molds that hung above the faded white cabinets. "A complete one-eighty. By the time I'm finished with it, you won't recognize it." Or so she hoped.

"You planning to sell?"

She shook her head. "I just need a change of pace."

"Is that why you're quitting your job at the vet clinic?" At her sharp glance, he added, "Hazards of a small town. I sent Matt in to pick up Scooter, he's our drug dog, and he heard you're supposed to up and quit."

That's what everyone expected her to do. She'd been passed over and humiliated. The old Jenna would have told Doc Morris where to go and how fast to get there.

Which is exactly why she'd bit her tongue and said nothing.

She wasn't going to tell him what a mistake he was making. Rather, she was going to show him.

By doing the right thing, being the right thing. For the first time in her life.

"I'm not quitting. It's just that there aren't any good equine facilities around, so I thought I'd revamp things here, add an extra barn, and the capacity to house horses. Then I'll be in a better position to help with the larger animals." Morris had her making house calls, but with her own facility, she could actually house the animals on the property and up their level of care. It was a fact he wouldn't be able to argue with or deny. There might be those who didn't want the likes of a Tucker on their property, but if she were in a position to provide the best care, well, even those stubborn Sawyers wouldn't be able to argue with that.

Speaking of the Sawyers . . .

Her gaze shifted to Hunter. While he didn't carry the name, he was still a Sawyer through and through. A direct descendant of Elijah Sawyer via his Mimi, Elijah's youngest daughter and Hunter's great-grandmother.

Clara Bell Sawyer was the only one of Elijah's offspring still alive. At ninety-four, she was one of the town's oldest citizens and the star of this year's pancake breakfast sponsored by the Rebel Rotary Club.

Hunter looked every bit a Sawyer with his dark hair and good looks. Only his eyes gave any clue that he was part DeMassi. They were a brighter shade of blue fringed in thick, dark lashes. The kind of eyes that sparkled and heated a woman from the inside out.

The last thought struck and she let loose a shaky breath. "I'm not quitting," she said again. "Just making some major changes."

"That's good."

"Let's hope." The words were out before she could stop them. He slid her a questioning expression before static shattered the sudden quiet and his attention shifted to the walkie-talkie.

"You want me to wait on you?" came the familiar male voice.

"Negative," Hunter said. "Take them to the station. I'll be right behind you. Again, I'm really sorry," he told her, his gaze catching and holding hers. "I'd really like to stop by tomorrow, if you don't mind."

"I . . . Listen, I know there's this vibe between us, but . . ."

"To take one more look around." The words faded into a small grin that sent a burst of warmth through her. "To see if James Harlin left anything lying around. Before the rafters come down."

"Oh, um, yeah. Sure. I'll be home tomorrow evening. Anytime after six. Unless we get an emergency call."

"Of course."

"But I might not be the one sent out. There's another vet at the clinic," she added. Okay, so she was running off at the mouth, telling Hunter DeMassi about the new vet and the very fact that she wasn't Dr. Morris's right hand anymore. "He's new. Dr. Morris just hired him because we've got a really busy workload."

"I can imagine."

"Not that I can't handle lots of work. I love being busy." She caught the next sentence before it could spill over and drew a deep breath. "I'm sorry. That's probably way too much information."

"It's fine." A grin tugged at the corner of his mouth and her stomach hollowed out. "I'll see you tomorrow night barring no emergencies."

"Sure."

Oh, boy.

She drew another deep breath and concentrated on closing the door behind him. So what if he was stopping by tomorrow night? It's not like he was coming to see *her*. He was still investigating her grandfather's death.

It was business. Strictly business.

She knew the feeling. She had plenty of her own to tend to. She eyed the boxes sitting here and there and reached for the nearest one.

A few minutes later, she was tossing more magazines onto the fire and praying for even the slightest breeze.

It was definitely going to be one long, hot night.

CHAPTER 5

"Let them go." Hunter handed the file to Chief Deputy Bobby Sawyer McGuire and motioned to the cell and the two men sitting on the bench behind the iron bars.

"You're kidding, right?" Bobby shook his head. "These two jokers shot up the Tucker place."

"It was just two bullets," one of the men offered. "Why, that ain't nothing a little spackle cain't fix."

"Put a sock in it," Bobby growled at the man before arching an eyebrow at Hunter. "Are you really serious?"

"They claim they were hunting and accidentally shot in the wrong direction." Hunter shrugged. "There are no other witnesses to dispute the claim, so let 'em go."

"Can't we at least charge them for trespassing?"

They could, but that would undermine Hunter's entire surveillance operation. His hunch had been right and the men hadn't seen who'd snuck up on them. They'd been chasing him, but they hadn't known for sure that it was him, and he meant to keep it that way. That meant no coming forward as an eyewitness. Even more, he couldn't very well keep tabs on their operation if there was no muscle to keep the still churning. No, he needed to let them go and proceed with the surveillance.

That, and he needed to keep an eye on Jenna Tucker.

"No one was home at the Tucker house," he said again, raising his voice a notch so as to make sure the two men heard, "so no one's pressing any charges. A good thing for you two." Hunter walked forward then, stopping just a foot shy of the cell door. "Those bullets could have done some serious damage if someone had been home."

"I'm telling you, Sheriff, it was an accident," Cole Mayweather grumbled. The man was in his midfifties, with snow-white hair and a mustache to match. "That hog climbed right up there on the front porch. I couldn't let him get away. Why, that sumbitch has been tearing up all my wife's tomato plants. I promised I'd bring him in for her. Ain't nobody gets away with poaching on my property."

"Damn straight," the other man offered. Monty Mayweather, Cole's younger brother by three years shrugged. "We almost had him, too." His gaze caught and held Hunter's.

No glimmer of recognition. No hint of awareness. Nothing to indicate that the person he'd seen out in the woods had been the local sheriff.

Then again, Hunter had worn civilian clothes for a reason. That, and the cover of darkness had saved his ass in a major way by concealing his identity. They'd only gotten a look at the back of his head.

This time.

He had no doubt that Cole and Monty would step up their precautions from here on out. Maybe even move their still site.

If it, indeed, belonged to them. They could just be the muscle behind the actual moonshiners.

While he wouldn't consider the middle-aged brothers much when it came to muscle, they had a hardness in their eyes that said they would gladly take down not just a hog, but anything else that crossed them.

He just wasn't so sure they were actually smart enough to be behind the brewing.

Maybe. Maybe not.

He shook his head, filing away the unanswered questions with the dozens of others that sailed in and out of his head. He had a lot more work to do if he wanted to blow the lid off their moonshine operation, and he couldn't do it with either man sitting in jail.

"Sheriff?" the female voice crackled over the mic pinned to his collar. "We've got a hostage situation."

"Come again?"

"I just got a call from Lorelei Sawyer. She said that Gerald was out picking figs off that tree that sits on the property line when Haywood Tucker climbed over the fence with a twelve-gauge shotgun."

"Don't tell me he shot Gerald?"

"Sort of."

"How do you *sort of* shoot someone?"

"He shot the heads off of two of his garden gnomes. Said he was going to do even worse to Gerald if he didn't let loose of *his* figs. Long story short, Gerald refused to give up the goods, Haywood aimed for another garden gnome that exploded and sent a piece of concrete flying. The concrete nearly decapitated Gerald's big toe. He's at the Urgent Care and Lorelei is here to file charges because Haywood is holed up in her greenhouse with her prize-winning roses."

"That was the short of it?"

"I could have mentioned that he put the remaining garden gnomes in some very interesting sexual positions while he was killing time in the greenhouse, waiting for justice as he called it, but I figured this was need-to-know only." At that moment, he heard Lorelei Sawyer's voice in the background as she sent up a vengeful prayer to God to strike Haywood dead with a lightning bolt, or at least blast a certain body part, in the name of the Father, the Son, and the ever-lovin' Holy Ghost, all three of which knew beyond a doubt that that fig tree was on Sawyer property.

"Tell her to head over to the Urgent Care to check on her husband. I'll take care of Haywood. You're damn lucky the Tuckers aren't pressing any charges," he said again, trying to convince both shiners that whoever they'd been chasing had been running for cover, not for home. The last thing he wanted was for Cole and Monty to think that Jenna was involved in any way. "And even luckier the house was empty."

"Yeah, yeah," Cole muttered. "We're the two luckiest sumbitches alive." He rolled his eyes. "Are we getting out anytime soon, hoss? I'd like to get home in time to watch Jimmy Fallon."

"Me, too," Monty chimed in. "I love Fallon. At the same time, I sure-as-shootin' wouldn't mind seeing you drag old Haywood out of that greenhouse and smack-dab into one of these cells." He grinned. "Ain't nothing better than seeing a Tucker get what's coming to him."

Hunter shrugged. "Then again, it *is* getting kind of late and you boys *were* trespassing . . ."

"Sorry, Sheriff," Cole blurted, throwing up his hands. "Don't worry about us. We're going straight home." He slapped a hand against Monty's chest. "Ain't that right, brother?"

"You bet."

He arched an eyebrow. "No detours?" Both men shook their heads profusely and he motioned to his deputy. "Open it up and get these boys out of here." Hunter turned on his heel and cast a glance at the storeroom that led to the back door and freedom. He tamped down on the sudden urge to run, to get the hell out of Dodge and never look back.

If only for a little while.

But a small taste would only make him want more and so he did what he always did—he headed for the front of the building and the SUV parked at the curb.

"Shouldn't you be sending someone else?" Marge asked as he passed the dispatch desk where she stood opposite a frazzled redhead wearing a REBEL COUNTY ROSE CLUB T-shirt and a vengeful expression.

"Bobby's busy processing paperwork. I'll take care of Haywood."

"But you've had your nose to the blacktop since the crack of dawn," Marge reminded him. "Why, I bet you haven't even ate a lick of supper."

"What can I say?" Hunter gave her a wink. "Duty calls." And he answered. He'd made that promise to the good citizens of the town when they'd elected him.

And to himself when he'd said good-bye to his baby brother and his own unreliable ways.

He just wished that keeping his vow, that doing the right thing for the first time in his life, didn't always feel so fucking *wrong*.

CHAPTER 6

". . . and then he set fire to the greenhouse after he blew Gerald Sawyer's foot clean off his leg," came the familiar voice of Ann Louise Sugardale, the silver-haired receptionist who'd been answering phones at the Rebel Veterinary Clinic for longer than Jenna had been alive.

Jenna walked into the main lobby as Miss Ann handed a Visa card back to a young woman who stood opposite the reception desk, a chocolate Lab puppy in one hand and her wallet in the other.

"Clean off?" The young woman's eyes widened as she slid her card into her purse and shoved it into her bag.

Miss Ann shook her head. "Not ne'er a ligament nor a tendon in sight." Her voice lowered just a notch as she added, "Just a bloody stump."

"That's terrible."

"That's a Tucker for you." Her gaze met Jenna's at that moment and she shrugged. "No offense, Doc. It's just, well, you know Haywood and his bunch."

Trash.

She didn't say it out loud. Not this time. Not since Jenna had chewed her a new one the last time she'd made a rude comment against the Tuckers.

Still, her pursed lips and wary gaze said it all. She was thinking it. She was also thinking that she ought to find an excuse to grab her purse and get while the getting was good.

Miss Ann knew Jenna's temper all too well.

"I really didn't mean nothing," the older woman started again, but Jenna held up a hand.

"It's all right, Miss Ann. If Haywood did something so awful, I'm sure he'll get what's coming to him."

The old woman's look of surprise was worth choking down the anger simmering inside. Almost. But then Miss Ann launched into a tirade about how Haywood had desecrated all of Lorelei Sawyer's garden statues, from her gnomes to a replica of the Mother Mary that sat atop a birdbath, and Jenna felt the anger roiling again.

But she wasn't giving in. Not this time.

Not ever again.

She drew a deep, shaky breath, turned her attention to the young boy sitting in a nearby chair and the pet squirrel clutched in his lap. "Looks like you're next, sweetie."

"It's Chipper." The boy motioned to his squirrel. "She's not eating like she usually does. My pa said she's sick." Worry furrowed his brow. "She's going to be okay, isn't she?"

"I'll do everything I can to make sure of that." She gave him a wink and stroked the animal's soft fur. "Why don't you come on back and let me have a look?"

She plucked the chart out of the tray on the counter

and motioned to a nearby exam room. A smile on her face, she followed the boy inside, effectively shutting off Miss Ann and her description of the now decapitated Mother Mary.

It's not about Miss Ann. It's about Chipper. Poor, possibly sick Chipper who needs your full and undivided attention.

"Now," she murmured as she closed the door and drew another deep breath. "Let's see what's going on."

The squirrel wasn't sick.

"She's pregnant," she told twelve-year-old Chase McIntyre a few minutes later.

The boy's face went from relieved to excited at the speed of light. "She's having babies?"

"It would seem so."

"How many?"

"There's no way to tell without an ultrasound, but I would make sure you have plenty of warm bedding because it could be quite a few. This breed is known for producing large litters."

"Why won't she eat?"

"She's probably feeling a little picky right now. They do that at first, but when she gets hungry enough, she'll start eating again. Make sure you give her plenty of food. And these supplements might help." She retrieved a small bottle from a nearby shelf. "Crush the pill into her food bowl."

"So that's it?"

"That's it."

He gave her a grin, revealing a mouthful of braces. "Thanks Dr. Tucker."

"Thank you for bringing her in." She finished making

notes in the chart and reached for the door. "Let's get you checked out."

Luckily, Miss Ann had lost her captive audience. Instead, she looked ready to lose her mind thanks to a crate full of chickens parked on top of the counter. "I can't just put them all in one chart. If you want the animals seen, they each count as a patient," she was trying to explain to an ancient-looking man in overalls.

"But it's one cage," Shorty Tucker pointed out. Along with Clara Bell Sawyer, Shorty was one of the oldest residents of Rebel, Texas, and Jenna's cousin three or four times removed. Or maybe he was a great-great-uncle.

She wasn't sure, she just knew they shared a bloodline somewhere along the way.

Unlike Clara Bell, Shorty still lived independently in a small house at the edge of town. He wore a pair of worn overalls as run-down as his house, a red-and-white VFW POST #202 cap, and an expression that said he wasn't backing down.

"Everybody knows chickens come in bunches," Shorty went on. "Ain't nobody got just one chicken on account of the raccoons pick 'em off one by one. A fella's got to get himself several chickens. It ain't about the chickens. It's about the cage. One cage. So it's one ticket."

"Says you," Miss Ann huffed. "*Ten* chickens, *ten* tickets."

"In *one* cage," Shorty insisted. "Hell's bells, woman, cain't you count?"

"Listen here, Shorty Tucker, I can count just fine. You're the one who can't seem to understand . . ." Ann went off into a carefully worded explanation about grade school and the fact that Shorty was older than Jesus, which explained why he didn't rightly remember his math lessons, which earned her an equally scathing response from the old man who pointed out that Jesus had passed her over when he'd been handing out manners and good looks.

Ann's gasp was so loud that Jenna actually thought about intervening, but then she smiled, plucked the next folder from the desk, and turned to the two Mini Plush Lop rabbits sitting nearby with their owner.

While she wasn't going to give Ann a piece of her mind, she wasn't going to deny Shorty the right to his.

"Hello Brad and Angelina," she murmured as she eyed the fluffy white rabbits before turning to the young woman holding their leashes. "Are we doing shots today?"

The woman nodded. "And I was hoping you could give Brad a little extra something. I want a litter of baby rabbits. I'm giving them to my nieces and nephews for Easter and time's running out. While the real Brad did just fine in that department, this one doesn't seem all that interested."

"We don't really do fertility treatments here. We like to let nature take its course."

"But I've had them in the same cage for six months and nothing. I don't think he's interested."

"I don't think he's a he," Jenna said as she picked up the first rabbit and took a look. "In fact, I'm positive. This is a female."

The woman's expression fell. What am I supposed to do with them now?"

"Take them home and love them?" Jenna offered.

The woman gave her a scathing look. "I don't love them. They were my Easter project. My sister-in-law gave out baby chicks last year and it's all my nieces and nephews have talked about since. I can't show up with some marshmallow Peeps now and look like the lame aunt again." She seemed to think. "Then again, I could get them these two-foot chocolate bunnies I saw online. Chocolate trumps a live animal, don't you think?"

"But what about Brad and Angelina, here?"

Claire gave her a hopeful expression along with the two leashes. "Surely you could hook them up with a good home? You're a vet, after all."

"I didn't mean to shoot off his toe. The old bastard got in my way, is all," Haywood Tucker said for the umpteenth time as Hunter led him into a cell and steered him to a nearby bench.

"You're lucky you didn't kill him."

"He's the lucky one." Haywood adjusted the ball cap on his bald head. "Lucky he didn't take a piece of concrete to the gut. Though I can't say as I would regret it if he had. He's been poaching my figs for six years now. It's about time he got what's coming to him."

"That tree isn't yours or his. The judge hasn't decided yet."

"He will and when he does I'll be due an apology for damned sure."

"The only thing that's coming to you is breakfast. You're in for the night."

"But Sheriff—"

"And all day if you can't post bail. Let Bobby know when you're ready to make your call." He locked the cell door, turned on his heel, and headed down the hall to his office. An oatmeal bar sat on a paper plate on his desk with a note from Marge that read *Eat already*.

He took a few bites and finished up the paperwork he'd left earlier that day before finally calling it a night.

The drive home took longer than it should have if he'd been headed to the small house that sat at the edge of town. Instead, he found himself feeling anxious. Restless. So Hunter hit the road leading out of town and opened up the gas a little. Air rushed through the windows, temporarily distracting him from the heat coiling inside him.

Thanks to the memory of Jenna's body so soft against his.

Christ, he was pathetic.

He'd been so busy with work that he hadn't had the time to drive to Austin and blow off a little steam. Something he couldn't do right here in town. He was the sheriff, after all. That meant no hooking up with just anyone. Folks looked to him to be an example. That meant no one-night stands. No, if he was going to hook up here in town it had to be with a woman who meant something to him. And he'd yet to find one.

Not that he'd been looking.

Hell, no. He had enough on his shoulders without adding the responsibility of a relationship to the mix.

No, he couldn't hook up with anyone in town. That meant driving somewhere else and he just hadn't had the time.

Or the energy.

He was full of it tonight. Enough to push him well past the county line. But instead of stopping off at Diamonds

& Denim, he left the neon lights in his rearview and turned onto the road leading out to the rodeo arena.

The motion was instinctive. Something he'd done so many times in the past that he never really gave it much thought.

Then.

But things were different now. He didn't belong out here anymore than he belonged on the back of a bucking bronc.

He wasn't that same man.

He couldn't be.

No matter how familiar the feelings pushing and pulling inside of him.

Fuck.

He hit the brakes and watched the spray of gravel as he swung the SUV around and headed back toward Rebel. He thought of stopping off to see his Mimi, but he knew it was well past her bedtime. Instead, he headed for the small two-bedroom Colonial just off Main Street.

Pulling into the driveway, he killed the engine and eyed the small front porch, the single bulb burning next to the door. He thought about going inside, climbing into bed and getting some much needed shut-eye, but he couldn't seem to move.

Instead, he leaned back and tipped his hat down over his eyes. And then he let his thoughts wander for just a few moments.

What it would be like to be just a man again.

One who could touch Jenna Tucker if and when he damn well pleased.

CHAPTER 7

"Don't be mad," Jenna said when she walked into the house to find a barking Jezebel waiting for her. The dog took one look at the two balls of white fluff in the cage and started growling. "I couldn't let Claire Westbrook toss them out of her Volvo on her way home, and you know that's what would happen. That woman doesn't have a nurturing bone in her body. Besides, it's not like they're competition. You're still my number-one dog." A bark drifted from outside and she added, "My number one Yorkie/poodle/grade-A mutt, that is." The whimpering outside quieted and she set the rabbit cage on the kitchen table before scooping up the white ball of canine fluff she'd brought home months ago from the veterinary clinic.

Jezebel had been a stray she'd found hurt and bleeding by the side of the road. She'd patched up the little dog and brought her back to the Tucker spread on a temporary basis. Until a good home could be found.

That had been over a year ago.

"Let's get you a treat," she murmured, grabbing a handful of Milk-Bones and a bag of Doritos. She was just about to head into the living room when her cell rang.

She sat Jez down and plucked the iPhone off the

kitchen table. The number registered Unavailable, but that was nothing new. She received tons of calls from worried pet owners, some of whom registered while others didn't. "Dr. Tucker," she said as she pressed the Answer button. "How can I help you?"

"Jenna?"

The man's familiar voice whispered through her head and her stomach tightened. Chuck Wallace had been her most recent breakup. They'd dated for a little over two months. He owned the local cleaners where she took the occasional DRY CLEAN ONLY label. He was average height. Medium brown hair. Decent looks. A nice enough guy. And that was the trouble in a nutshell.

He was nice.

Which was why she'd gone out with him in the first place. But then she'd realized that hopping from man to man, even a nice man, wasn't helping her reputation in the slightest.

She'd told him she couldn't see him again, and then he'd asked her to marry him.

He'd been asking ever since, even though she'd made it perfectly clear that she didn't like him like that. They'd slept together once and while it hadn't been all that great for her, he couldn't seem to let it go. She was The One. At least that's what the card on the last flower arrangement had said. And the frosting on the vanilla sheet cake he'd had delivered to the clinic last month. And the sky-writing crop duster that had painted the sky white just this past weekend.

"Listen, Chuck. I know you think I'm going to change my mind, but I'm not. It's over." She gathered her courage. "You're not the guy for me."

"You say that, but you haven't gone out with anyone else since we broke up. That says something, Jenna."

It said she was turning over a new leaf, but Chuck wasn't getting the message.

"I'm not interested in dating anyone."

"That's what you say, but a woman like you needs a man. You deserve one."

"I don't need a man. I'm too busy for a relationship."

"You don't have to play hard to get, Jenna. You've got me. I'm hooked."

"I don't want you, Chuck. You're a great guy, but—"

"You don't have to flatter me. I'm all yours, honey. I'm head over heels. Yours for the taking."

So much for just giving it to him straight, which is what Callie had always told her. She'd finally started taking her eldest sister's advice, but it wasn't getting her anywhere. The guy wasn't listening.

"I can't even think straight," he rushed on. "Do you know I shoved a silk cardigan into the washing machine and steamed Mr. Merriweather's wash-and-wear leisure suit? I don't know whether I'm coming or going, Jenna. I need to see you—"

"Beeeeeeeeep," she cut in, doing her best imitation of an incoming call. It was a lame move, but she was desperate. "Sorry, Chuck. I've got to take this. It's an emergency."

"But—"

She hit the Off button and set the phone down. It rang again, the Unavailable flashing, and she sent the call to her voice mail.

She ignored a rush of guilt—she'd tried to let him down easy—and snatched up her snacks. She'd wasted too much time on too many guys who weren't right for her because of guilt. Because they really were all great guys and it seemed such a shame to cut them loose simply because she didn't feel *it*.

That breath-stealing, bone-melting rush of heat that she'd felt when she'd climbed onto the back of that motorcycle with bad boy number one all those years ago.

The thought conjured a memory of hard muscle pressing her down into the kitchen floor, bullets whizzing overhead. Her nerves tingled and her nipples pebbled and . . .

She shook away the memory. There'd been no *it* with Hunter DeMassi. He was the sheriff, for heaven's sake. A pillar of the community. Far from the wild, rebellious bad boys she'd gotten hooked on in her youth.

What she'd felt last night had been a fluke. Any normal, healthy, red-blooded female who'd been on the wagon for as many months as she'd been would have had the same reaction. She'd simply been so close and he'd been, well, a lot more muscular than his uniform usually let on. His shoulders broad. His arms ripped with muscle. And the smell . . . There'd been something oddly dangerous.

Um, yeah. The moment, remember? The gunshots? The bullets?

It hadn't been the man himself who'd hollowed out her stomach and made her want to throw her arms around him and kiss him for all she was worth.

Circumstance.

The subject closed, she grabbed her snacks and headed for the living room. Depositing everything on the coffee table, she flipped on the ancient console television. The screen blazed to life, shifting from green to red before settling somewhere in between for the watered-down color. "We've got to get a new one."

A new everything, she reminded herself as she turned and headed back to the kitchen for a drink. She retrieved a soda from the avocado-green refrigerator and set it on the old scarred Formica counter.

Old. Scarred. That described the entire house and all that was in it. The place was full of the original furnishings that had been there when Jenna and her family had moved in with her grandpa all those years ago.

They'd done it to help him out, but Jenna knew that her own father had needed help as well. While Rose and James Junior had given their daughters plenty of love when they'd been alive, they hadn't showered them with much else. Her father had been a ranch hand who'd traveled here and there, taking jobs where he could find them until he'd finally moved back to Rebel with his wife and three daughters. He'd settled into his childhood home to look after his father who'd taken a nosedive straight into a jar of moonshine after his wife's death years before.

James Harlin hadn't come up for air in all the time that had followed. Until he'd lost his son and daughter-in-law in a car accident. He'd cut down then not because he'd wanted to straighten up and take care of his granddaughters, but because Callie had made him.

Jenna's eldest sister had flushed every drop of shine down the toilet as fast as James Harlin could brew it up. That hadn't kept him from indulging, but it had slowed him down a little.

Enough that he hadn't been such a mean SOB all the time.

She stiffened against the sudden softening in her chest. So what if he hadn't been a total dick twenty-four/seven? He'd still been a major ass ninety-nine point nine percent of the time and she wasn't going to waste her tears on him.

Her eldest sister had fought some demons where James Harlin was concerned and while Jenna knew Callie had made peace with her past, she wasn't going to betray her sister by mourning a man who'd rarely had a kind word for his own flesh and blood.

Even if he had let her sit with him and watch *Family Feud* instead of doing her homework while Callie and Brandy had been at their after-school jobs. And then there'd been the time that he'd picked her up at the middle school because she'd nailed Darla Sue Chantilly in the mouth with a dodgeball for calling her a white trash Tucker.

He hadn't come in apologizing like Callie usually did. No, James had marched in there as proud as you please, told the principal and Darla Sue's parents where they could stick it, and had a good chuckle when Jenna had given him the play-by-play of what had gone down after Darla had called her the name in front of the entire girl's sixth grade gym class. He'd laughed himself pink and then bought her an ice cream sandwich at the Pac-n-Save.

The memory rose up as she opened the freezer and spotted the familiar box of frozen treats stuffed in the back.

He'd always had a thing for ice cream sandwiches.

He'd eaten one every night before bed. When he hadn't been drinking, of course.

She balled her fingers and moved around a few packs of frozen vegetables and an ancient half-empty ice tray. James Harlin was gone now and she was no longer the same rambunctious girl she'd once been. She was a full-grown woman and she was conducting herself as such. That meant no more bad behavior.

And no more ice cream sandwiches.

She found the quart of raspberry sorbet she'd picked up at the store a few days before and closed the freezer. Grabbing a spoon from a nearby drawer, she headed back into the living room and sank down onto the couch next to Jez.

"Let's see who gets a rose tonight." She handed Jez a Milk Bone, popped the lid on the sorbet, and sank her spoon deep. The first bite went down cold and smooth just as a knock sounded on the door.

Chuck. Would the guy never give up?

She shoved another bite into her mouth as she got to her feet. She grabbed the doorknob just as a burst of white hot pain hit her temples and she grimaced.

"I really appreciate the thought, but it can't happen between us," she said as she yanked open the door. "You just don't turn me on. You'll never turn me on. *Never.*"

"Is that so?" came the deep, rumbling voice.

She blinked through the pain and found herself staring into Hunter DeMassi's bluer-than-blue eyes. Her throat closed on an explanation and it was all she could do just to breathe as his full lips hinted at a wicked grin that did sinful things to her heart.

"Never say never, sugar."

CHAPTER 8

Wicked?

There was nothing wicked about Hunter DeMassi or his grin.

That's what she told herself as she sat in her living room and tried to ignore the man hammering at her front door. He'd brought a few two-by-fours to nail up inside to cover the holes until he could bring out a new door.

She'd protested that everything was going to get tossed out anyway with the renovation—after she'd given a lengthy explanation that she'd thought he was someone else when she'd answered the door—but he'd insisted on the repair.

"Toss it out when the time comes, it doesn't matter." He'd shrugged his broad shoulders. "I promised to fix it and that's what I'm doing." He'd winked then. "And if this guy Chuck doesn't ring your bell, you're right to cut him loose."

"My show's on," she'd blurted, eager to escape the strange glimmer in his eyes.

A look that said he knew exactly how to ring her bell if given half the chance.

Crazy.

This was Hunter DeMassi. Public servant extraordi-
naire. Pillar of the community.

He didn't ring bells. He spent his time keeping law
and order and helping out with the middle school car
wash and judging pies for the annual ladies' auxiliary
bake-off. He was a stand-up guy. Wholesome. Nice.

With one sexy, wicked-as-all-get-out grin.

The notion struck and she reached for the sorbet. She
swallowed a mouthful. The pain of another brain freeze
splintered her temples and killed the crazy thought.

Sexy and wicked?

Hunter?

She was losing it.

Grabbing the remote, she hit the volume and pushed
it louder to drown out the hammering coming from the
doorway. Her gaze fixed, she did her best to concentrate
on the good-looking guy handing out roses.

He came up short and the girl left without a flower
burst into tears.

Definitely melodrama. The guy was cute in his
tuxedo, but he looked too . . . good.

No scuffed-up boots or ripped jeans or kiss-my-ass
attitude.

The kind that really got Jenna going.

Her weakness, or it had been back before she'd made
up her mind to clean up her act.

"That'll do it for now." The deep voice drew her attention to the doorway and the man who stood there but-
toned up in his crisply ironed uniform, his regulation
black shoes polished to a nice sheen.

Nice, she reminded herself.

A fact she would have been able to remember except

that it was late and a five o'clock shadow had crept across his broad jaw. His hair was slightly disheveled and if she hadn't known better, she would have sworn he'd just rolled out of bed . . .

Wait a second. What the hell was she doing?

She was *not* lusting after the local sheriff.

She held tight to the vow, killed the volume on the television, and pushed to her feet. "You really didn't have to go to so much trouble."

"No trouble. It's the least I could do after scaring the crap out of you last night." He glanced at the remaining boxes that littered the entryway. "More to burn?"

"Those are getting picked up by the local shelter, but I'm sure I'll have some more things for a fire by the time I'm finished. I was just killing a little time before tackling the upstairs. They're going to be demolishing the house next week."

"So soon?"

"The sooner the better." He didn't say anything for a long moment. Instead, he just stared at her as if he didn't buy the comment. "This house really is an accident waiting to happen. It's falling apart at the seams."

"It could definitely use a little work." He eyed the peeling wallpaper. "At the same time, there's something to be said for a house that's stood this long. When was this place built? Seventy, eighty years ago?"

"Eighty-eight."

"And you're going to tear it down and start from scratch just like that?"

"Why not?"

He shrugged. "Because it's got character."

"I guess it does," she said, eyeing the wooden floor

and deep gouge that she'd made with one of the roller skates she'd bought with her birthday money when she'd turned ten. Her sisters had scraped together most of it, but then she'd come up short and James Harlin had offered up the five dollar gold piece he'd kept in his top drawer.

He hadn't made a big deal out of it. He hadn't even said a word. He'd just left the coin on her pillow and since he'd never been much for anyone making a fuss, she'd kept her thanks to herself.

Instead, she'd laced up her skates and sailed down the hall, past his bedroom so that he could see her and how happy he'd made her, and straight into a nearby wall. The edge of the skate had dug into the floor when she'd tried to break her fall and left a mark that had been there ever since.

She'd sprained her ankle that day, but it had been worth it. For those few moments, she'd felt invincible gliding down the hall on her new skates courtesy of the most important people in her life. She'd felt special. *Loved.*

"It's not such a bad house." She stiffened against the sudden warmth inside of her. "But it's cheaper to start fresh than try to renovate." Tearing down the house was the practical thing to do.

The right thing.

Which was why she'd made the decision in the first place. She was through acting on emotion. Been there, done that. No more.

"I really should get to work," she started, eager to ignore the strange feelings pushing and pulling at her. The past with her granddad.

The present with Hunter and his see-all blue eyes.

"I could help," he offered.

See? Nice.

Her gaze hooked on the dark shadow of his jaw. His eyes seemed brighter somehow, understanding, and her stomach hollowed out.

"No, no," she finally managed when she found her voice. "You've done enough."

"It's no problem. I'm already here and I've got a little time before I check in back at the station." He reached for the mic on his collar. "Marge, this is Hunter. I'll be out at the Tucker place if you need me."

"Roger that, Sheriff," came the female voice. "And don't forget to eat that snack I packed in your glove compartment if you know what's good for you."

"Yes, ma'am."

Jenna arched an eyebrow. "I thought Marge was the dispatcher, not your mother."

"She thinks I need to eat better. I guess a slice of cold pizza and a bag of chips doesn't work for her."

"I know the feeling," Jenna said, glancing at her phone and the message light that blinked. "Callie's been on me lately, too, since she moved out." She motioned to the sorbet. "I'm supposed to be making healthier choices but I just can't seem to shake the Doritos."

"Corn is a vegetable."

His grin was infectious and for the next few seconds she found herself wondering what it would feel like to rub her finger across the roughness of his cheek. To feel that friction on her hand. Her neck. Her breasts . . .

"Time to get to work," she blurted. "I really don't need any help."

"I won't take no for an answer."

"You really don't have anything better to do than help me?"

"I'm a public servant. That's what I do."

He certainly wasn't offering because he was just as turned on as she was.

Her head knew that, but damned if her body had gotten the message. Her skin tingled and her muscles tensed and her lips twitched.

Just get it over with.

That's what her gut said.

Kiss him and you'll see it isn't all that great and then you can stop acting like a sex-starved idiot.

Because that's the way it always was with the nice guys like Hunter DeMassi. She'd tried it, hoping to turn the mild spark into a freaking inferno, to find a good guy that turned her on as much as the bad boys in her past, but it always fizzled out way too fast and she was left with a big fat nothing.

Just a guy that she wasn't the least bit attracted to who sent her flowers and candy and declared his love via crop duster.

Guys like Chuck. And Kevin. And Johnny. And Marty. And Spencer.

Ugh . . . No wonder the entire town thought she was a hoochie. She had way too many men in her past.

So what's one more? Just go for the smooch and get it over with so you can get back to work.

Stepping forward, Jenna reached him in a split-second and then she did what she'd been wanting to do since she'd first opened the door that night.

She threw her arms around him and kissed him.

CHAPTER 9

Hunter DeMassi had been kissed by a hell of a lot of women over the years.

But none had ever felt quite like this.

Like *her*.

Jenna's soft, full lips covered his. Her hands came up to clutch at his shoulders. She canted her head and licked the seam of his mouth.

Instinct kicked in and he opened up before he could think better of it. Her tongue dipped inside and touched his and his initial shock faded in a wave of raw, consuming hunger. It had been so long and she felt so good. He'd been on the wagon for too many months now, contenting himself with a few fantasies in the dead of night because he wasn't about to kill his reputation by hooking up with one of the women down at the local bar. But it wasn't enough to satisfy him completely. He needed something more. Something real.

Her.

He leaned into her, pressing her up against the nearby wall. His hands slid around her waist. His fingers pressed into the lush curve of her bottom, drinking in the warmth of her body that seeped through the thin material of her T-shirt. The cedar planks were cool against the backs of his hands, but it did little to soothe the heat that rushed through him like a spark through a field of dry, rain-deprived grass.

A soft moan vibrated from her mouth as she curled her hands up around his neck, her fingers insistent at the base of his skull. Her legs shifted slightly apart, cradling the hard-on that throbbed to life beneath the fly of his beige slacks.

His cock pushed, desperate to feel the warmth of her skin as he explored the cavern of her mouth. His tongue tangled with hers, probing and tasting. She was sweet. So deliciously sweet.

And hot.

He pulled her even closer and deepened the kiss, drinking her in like a man starved for water after an afternoon spent breaking the toughest bronc. But he couldn't get enough of her. She wasn't close enough and so he held her tighter. He couldn't taste enough and so he kissed her even deeper, longer. His heart pounded and his nerves buzzed and his fingers itched to slip beneath the waistband of her shorts and feel her warm, damp flesh pulse against his fingertips.

"You taste so sweet," he gasped against her lips.

"It's the sorbet," she breathed.

"It's you." His mouth covered hers again as his hands slid around to plunge beneath the hem of her shirt. He cupped her lace-covered breasts. Her nipple jutted through in one spot and rasped the center of his palm.

She moaned into his mouth and her body arched. Her hard, hot nipple pressed forward, greedy for more.

For sex.

The wild and wicked kind that made him want to take her right now up against the wall. No time to shed their clothes. Just her with her shorts tossed aside, her body warm and wet and welcoming. Him with his pants down around his ankles, his cock hard and greedy. Marge with her voice loud and grating, lecturing in his ear . . .

The thought stalled as the old woman's voice echoed, bouncing off the walls and shattering the haze of lust that surrounded them.

"We just got a call from Marvin VanSickle. He said Gerald's in the store looking at buckshot. He thinks he's stocking up to go after Haywood. To give him tit-for-tat."

Hunter tore his lips from Jenna's and her eyes popped open.

"What's wrong . . ." she started, but the words died as Marge's voice echoed again.

"Sheriff? You there?"

"Yeah," he said, pressing the button on his lapel. "I'm here. Send Bobby over to the sporting goods store to see what's really going on. I'll be right behind him."

"Roger that," she said and the radio went silent.

Tamping down on the disappointment welling inside him, he stared down at the woman slumped against the wall. Her lips were full and swollen, her eyes wide and shimmery. Worry furrowed her brow and his gut tightened.

"It's okay. We'll get there before they kill each other."

"Who?" His voice seemed to snag her attention. She shook her head. "What?"

"Gerald and Haywood. Relax." His fingers kneaded into her shoulder. "I won't let them kill each other."

"What?" She shook her head again, "Oh, yeah. You should go and keep them from doing anything stupid."

"I can come back later and give you a hand . . ."

"No, no. You go. I've got it covered here. Go," she added, her voice firmer. Licking her lips, she seemed to gather her control. "And thanks."

His gaze hooked on her mouth, on the soft tremble of her bottom lip and his throat went dry. Either it had been way too long since he'd had a good kiss, or she was a helluva lot better at it than most. "Thank *you*," he murmured. "You started it."

"I was talking about the door."

"I wasn't." He grinned before planting another quick kiss on her quivering lips. And then he turned and walked away before he did something really stupid.

Like touch her again.

Or kiss her.

Or fuck her.

And that would be so bad because?

It wouldn't have been if he'd been the same man he'd been years ago.

And she'd been the same woman.

While she'd been talking about the house, he had the gut feeling that she wanted to change more than just her surroundings, even if she had been the one to kiss him first.

It was just a hunch, but it kept him walking anyway. Hunter knew how hard it was to walk the straight and narrow. He sure as hell wasn't going to be the one to derail her.

Not yet, that is.

But if she tried kissing him again . . . Well, a man could only take so much.

CHAPTER 10

WTF?

She'd kissed him.

Of all the crazy, ridiculous, regrettable things she'd done in her lifetime. From climbing onto the back of Mack Connally's restored Harley and losing her virginity to the baddest boy in high school at the tender age of fifteen. To telling off old lady Bertha Walters Sawyer in the middle of last year's Founder's Day picnic because she had refused to eat the potato salad that Callie—aka a *Tucker*—had brought. And all the rash stunts in between.

She'd kissed *him.*

Not that it would have been any better if he'd kissed her. It was the kissing, itself, that posed the biggest threat.

Okay, so it wasn't the kissing. There was nothing wrong with kissing. Kissing was fine. Great. No, the problem here was that she'd *liked* kissing him.

She'd liked it too damned much.

Her lips tingled and her mind raced and her hands shook.

Kissing him should have been a huge letdown. The way it had been with Chuck. And before that, Kevin.

And Stan. And the half-dozen other nice guys she'd done her damnedest to fall in love with. The anticipation was always there. The hope that lightning would strike and bells would ring and the angels would sing and finally, *finally,* she would find *it* with a decent guy instead of some noncommittal bad boy.

But they'd all been a huge letdown.

That's what tonight should have been. That's why she'd done it in the first place. To give herself a big reality check.

But then she'd kissed him and now she wanted to do it again.

Uh-oh.

The doom whispered through her and denial kicked in.

Damn straight she wanted to do it again. She was crazy horny. Past the point of rational thought. Beyond reason. She could have kissed a poodle in her current state and she'd have sworn it was Ryan Reynolds/Brad Pitt/the super-hot guy who bagged groceries at the Piggly Wiggly and rode a Harley.

It wasn't Hunter DeMassi, himself.

Hell, no.

Guys like the sheriff—the kind, thoughtful, door-fixing kind—didn't press her buttons. She didn't lie awake thinking and fantasizing and *wanting* one when she should be sleeping.

Sleep?

Fat chance she decided later that night as she lay awake and stared at the ceiling.

She tossed the covers to the side, climbed out of bed, and headed for the cluttered attic.

A half-hour passed and she finished boxing up the pile of fifty-year-old newspapers that filled one corner of the massive room and turned to the stack of suitcases and trunks that sat nearby.

Grabbing one dusty leather trunk, she set it on the floor, popped the latch, and flipped open the lid. Hinges groaned and dust billowed. She blinked against a sudden burning and stared at the contents. A mess of clothes. Some shoes. An old baby doll. A pair of ancient reading glasses . . .

The list went on as she unearthed each item and either tossed it into her KEEP box, or the one that read TOSS.

If she couldn't sleep, and she certainly couldn't go back for seconds, then she had to *do* something.

"Last I heard it wasn't against the law for a man to buy bullets."

"A case of bullets," Deputy Bobby Sawyer McGuire pointed out, motioning to the boxes stacked on the glass countertop above a display of handguns.

"Nine boxes," Gerald Sawyer insisted, "is not an entire case of bullets. Why, it's a full box shy."

"One measly box is nothing. What could you possibly need nine boxes of bullets for?"

"Not that it's any of your damned beeswax," Gerald told the officer, "but Lorelei just bought a new SUV."

"And?"

"And we're talking top-of-the-line Lincoln Navigator with a touch screen and heated seats. You know how much extra I had to pay for those seats?"

"What do heated seats have to do with bullets?"

"Hold your britches. I'm getting there. See, the SUV is black," he announced, as if that said it all.

"And?

"I've got more than a dozen oak trees hanging over the driveway. That means birds. And lots of birds means lots of bird shit. And lots of bird shit means I won't just be washing that blasted Navigator on my day off. I'll be rinsing it off at least a few times a week. Maybe more. I cain't very well do that in my condition." He indicated the bandaged foot stuffed into a flip-flop. "I can barely walk, so I figured I'd just sit on my porch and take care of the bird situation. A few hundred rounds into those trees and it's bye, bye, birdie."

"So all this is just so you can shoot birds?"

"Not the birds themselves. I'm shooting at the trees, which stirs up a ruckus, which gets rid of the birds."

Bobby's gaze narrowed. "That's it? All this is just to clear out your trees?"

"Damn straight it is."

The deputy's gaze narrowed. "And you're not even the slightest bit anxious for a little payback where Haywood is concerned?"

"If I wanted to give that no-good Tucker what was coming to him, I'd toss one of them grenades I brought back from Iraq through his front door. Blow off a few body parts the way he did me. Come to think of it, that ain't a half bad idea—"

"Forget it," Hunter cut in. "Haywood's already in custody. There's no need for grenades."

"Or damn near a case of bullets," the deputy added. "You don't seriously think we're buying this whole bird shit business, do you?"

"It's the God's honest." Gerald crossed his heart and tried to look devout. "Though it does say in the Bible that vengeance is mine."

"God's the one doing the talking in the Bible," Bobby countered. "That means, he's the one carrying out the vengeance."

"That's one way to interpret it, I s'pose."

"That's the only way."

"Says you. It really depends on who is talking."

"God's talking," Bobby insisted again.

"Not right now. I'm talking, so *mine* refers to me. Yours truly. The Big G. And whose side are you on, anyway? Last I looked, you're every bit a Sawyer. The both of you. You ought to be taking up for me."

"We're on the side of the law," Hunter said.

"That's right," Bobby added. "We took an oath, and don't be thinking just because your last name is Sawyer that you're above the law. We're on to you and—"

"Let him be," Hunter said, glancing at the receipt the clerk had handed him when he'd first walked in. So Gerald had forked over a little too much just to get rid of a few birds? The man could still be telling the truth. And even if he wasn't, Haywood was in custody so he was safe should Gerald have an ulterior motive. "Make sure you watch where you're shooting," he told the man. "It's too early for hunting season when it comes to dove and quail. You wouldn't want yourself facing a stiff fine for an illegal kill. Maybe even some jail time."

"Not to worry, Sheriff. I been shooting since I was knee-high. This is all just to make some noise."

"I'd watch that, too, if I were you. Otherwise I'll have to haul you in for disturbing the peace."

"Why you'd just let him go?" Bobby asked when Gerald muttered a curse, grabbed his ammo, and walked out. "You know good and well he's out to scare more than just a few birds."

"Maybe, but at this point, it's just speculation. We can't arrest a man for something he *might* do and it certainly isn't against the law to buy ammunition in the state of Texas." He stared through the window, through the creeping dusk as the man hobbled around his pickup parked at the curb. A few seconds later, the engine grumbled to life and the lights flicked on. Tires squealed, a tailpipe sputtered, and Gerald disappeared down the street.

"He wanted two cases," Petey James Walker offered. The clerk shook his head. "But Arlo Gentry came in earlier today and wiped me out of everything save those nine boxes. He's got himself a coon problem."

"Coons?" Bobby arched an eyebrow. "I hate those little buggers."

"Nasty sons-a-bitches," Petey agreed. "Why, I had one kept getting into my rabbit pen—"

"If Gerald comes back for more," Hunter cut in, eager to kill the coon talk and get back to business, "give me a call, would you?"

"Sure thing, Sheriff. You really think he's going after Haywood?"

Hunter shrugged, but deep in his gut he already knew the answer. If this had been a minor disagreement between anyone else, he would have said hell no. Folks were smarter than that. Forgiving. But this was the Tuckers and the Sawyers. The last squabble between the warring factions had ended with a glass eye for Monty

Tucker because Brewster Sawyer had inadvertently shot it out while aiming for a hog, or so he claimed, and a prosthetic testicle for Brewster because Monty had fired back at his enemy's most cherished body part while aiming for that same hog—or so he'd said. Luckily, all the blood had made Monty's aim a fraction off and he'd merely taken off one of the twins instead of the man's penis, and all because of an argument that had started out innocently enough when Brewster's girlfriend had called Monty's wife a know-it-all at Wednesday night bingo.

When it came to the two warring families, things had a way of escalating. Fast.

The thought struck and Hunter found himself thinking about Jenna. And the kiss. And the way his libido had gone from zero to sixty in two seconds flat.

He hadn't meant to kiss her. In fact, he'd been damned intent on not kissing her. Or touching her. Or doing anything because, well, Hunter kept things strictly business whether he was on the clock or not.

But then she'd been close and he'd been horny and, well, the two had made for a deadly combination.

"You'd better head home," Hunter told Bobby.

"What about you?"

"I've got a few things to wrap up at the station."

"You want to come by the house for dinner?"

He arched an eyebrow at his deputy. "Lori's cousin wouldn't happen to be at this dinner, now, would she?" Bobby's wife had been trying to fix Hunter up with her cousin for the past six months. He'd effectively dodged each and every fix, but it was getting harder and harder because he was the sheriff and he didn't want to be rude.

"There's always a chance Kaitlyn might stop by. She and Lori are attached at the hip."

Which was the main reason Bobby was all for finding Kaitlyn her own man. He wanted his new bride of only nine short months all to himself and while her best friend was still single, that was next to impossible. He still had to deal with girls' night out. And pedicure Saturdays. And *Game of Thrones* watch parties.

"Kaitlyn's a great girl," Bobby added. "You really ought to give her a chance. She's a great cook. And she teaches Sunday school."

"I don't really have time tonight. Maybe next time."

Kaitlyn *was* perfect, and maybe it was high time he started dating. Maybe then he wouldn't be so all-fired anxious to kiss a woman he hardly knew.

"Definitely next time," he added.

Bobby nodded and headed out to his cruiser while Hunter climbed into the beige SUV parked nearby.

He needed to spend some of the sexual energy boiling inside of him and if that meant settling down with someone in town in order to do it, then so be it. He'd have dinner with Kaitlyn.

Later.

Right now, he still had work to do.

CHAPTER 11

Bud's Beer Garden was little more than a run-down shack off of Route 416. Tucked away behind a cluster of oak trees, the place had poor visibility from the main road and worse, it wasn't even on a Google map.

Mostly because the folks that hung out at Bud's were looking to stay off the grid. From hard-core bikers wanting to avoid the weekend warriors who filled the interstate bars, to a certain trio of moonshine runners eager to keep a low profile during their downtime, Bud's provided a safe haven to suck down beer, hustle pool, and pick up women.

Hunter knew that firsthand because it had been his go-to spot when he'd first started walking the straight and narrow. A place to escape from prying eyes for a few precious moments before duty called. But then Bud's had become more a reminder of what he'd left behind than a reprieve and so he'd stopped cutting loose altogether and gone cold turkey.

He shook off a niggle of regret and pulled into the gravel parking lot. He swerved into a spot off to the left of the building near a beat-up red Chevy pickup and a dusty black Harley, and killed the engine.

The place was a single-story metal building with a wooden porch that wrapped around the front. Old-fashioned swinging doors filled the doorway. A blue neon Bud's sign hung a few feet above. Dozens of beer posters filled the grime-covered windows and left little room for light to stream from the inside. Forget anything from this century as far as music went. The sound of Conway Twitty crooning about Linda drifted from inside. It was an oldie but goodie, like all the other throwback tunes that filled the ancient jukebox inside. Even more proof that things didn't change much in a small town. Bud, himself, had started the place a long, long time ago when his wife Edna had picked up and left him for an encyclopedia salesman. He'd needed a distraction from an empty house and so he'd sold the place and turned to tequila and crying country songs to fill his spare time. Bud's had been in business ever since.

His gaze shifted to the silver Dodge Challenger sitting a few spaces away. The car was an older model that had certainly seen better days. There was a small dent in the front fender, a tiny crack in the left corner of the window, and a dozen other scratches here and there. Nothing special to look at, but then that was the point. It wasn't the exterior that mattered. Hunter knew there was a brand-spanking-new Challenger Hellcat engine under that hood. The fastest of its kind that could go zero to sixty in 3.5 seconds.

He knew because he'd chased the sonofabitch a time or two, not that he'd ever caught up to it. Or the man who sat behind the wheel.

If he wanted to catch up to legendary moonshine runner Gator Hallsey, a third-generation hauler who delivered shine all across the Lone Star state just like his dad and granddad before him, he had to do it here at Bud's. During the man's off time.

"A little out of your element, aren't you, Sheriff?" came the deep voice when he stepped up onto the wrap-around.

He peered into the darkness just to his right and made out the familiar shape of a man, a cigarette in his hand and a woman leaning against his side. He was tall with broad shoulders and blond hair that touched the collar of his blue button-down, the shirttails hanging loose. The butt of his Marlboro glowed like a laser beam in the shadowy darkness. A click sounded and the woman lit her own cigarette, her red lips drawing on the tip.

"Actually, this is exactly my element," Hunter told the man after tipping his hat to the woman. "I've sucked down my fair share of beers right here."

"I forget you used to be a bad ass way back when." Ryder Jax grinned, the expression splitting the darkness before he drew on the cigarette. The butt glowed even brighter. Smoke filled the air, along with the woman's laughter.

Ryder was also a moonshine runner. The second member of the infamous trio, and more importantly, Gator's right hand.

And damn near just as fast.

Fast enough to keep his ass out of jail and his record all but clean. The only thing that had ever been pinned on him were a few misdemeanors. Some minor traffic violations. And a restraining order filed by an ex-wife who claimed he'd broken into her house and threatened her.

In actuality, he'd broken into the house to claim his blue heeler, which she'd refused to hand over when she'd kicked his ass out for cheating. But the judge had been female and a cat lover, and so she'd ruled against him and signed the order.

Now Ryder couldn't go within one hundred feet of the ex or the dog.

"A shame you turned over a new leaf," Ryder added. "You were a lot more fun back in the day."

And a helluva lot more dangerous.

He'd tossed down too much booze and slept with too many women and thrown way too many punches.

The notion sent a burst of adrenaline through him and he stiffened. "Is Gator inside?"

Ryder shrugged. "That depends."

"On what?"

"Why you're here. If you're here on official business, then I'd have to say no. I ain't seen him all week. Maybe even all month."

"And if I'm not?"

"Then he might be inside counting the five hundred bucks he just won off me in a game of pool." The grin split the darkness again and the butt beamed a fiery red as he took another drag.

Hunter stepped toward the swinging doors. "Stay out of trouble."

"Always." Ryder grinned and dropped what was left of the Marlboro. The scuffed toe of his boot ground the butt into the gravel. "Let's get out of here," he told the woman standing next to him.

"It's about time." She pushed away from the wall and

dropped her own cigarette. "Let's head back to my place."

"Lead the way, darlin'. Lead the way."

Hunter watched the couple cross the parking lot, headed for the jacked-up pickup truck that sat off to the far left before turning toward the doorway.

The stench of stale beer and cigarette smoke swallowed him up as he walked inside. He blinked, his eyes adjusting to the bright neon that cut through the darkness.

A dozen or so bodies filled the interior. A few leather-clad men sat at the bar, sucking down shots of Jack Daniel's. There were more scattered among the tables, some playing cards, some eyeing the women who filled the perimeter. Hunter recognized a handful of faces from town. Most of them divorcées out looking for a second shot at excitement. There were a few single women, but they weren't the type that vied for his company at the weekly church picnic.

Those good, wholesome types wouldn't be caught dead in a place like this.

Another quick visual of the interior and his attention settled on the pool table in the far corner and the man leaning over, lining up his next shot.

He wore a black V-neck T-shirt that stretched tight over his broad shoulders and revealed some heavily ripped biceps and a pair of worn jeans. He had dark hair pulled back in a loose ponytail and a few days' worth of beard covering his face. A half-empty bottle of Fireball whiskey sat on the edge of the table, next to a wad of cash.

He leaned over, aimed, and took his shot. The ball shot forward, clashing into a red solid and sending it straight into a nearby pocket with a swift *whoosh*.

The man across the table let loose a string of cussing before grumbling, "I need another beer if I'm going to get my ass handed to me again." And then he turned and headed for the bar.

"So what do you want?" Gator asked when Hunter reached him.

"What makes you think I want anything?"

"You always want something." Gator's bright blue eyes swept Hunter from head to toe. "Though you're usually in uniform. What's with the civilian clothes?"

"I didn't want to spook anyone." That, and he'd tried to go home first. To settle in for the night and forget all about Jenna and the kiss and the damning fact that he hadn't given one single thought to what he'd been doing. He'd been acting on instinct. Feeling.

Just like way back when.

"The uniform is dirty," Hunter said. "Listen, we picked up Cole and Monty Mayweather yesterday for illegal hunting." When Gator arched an eyebrow, he added, "They fired off some rounds and hit a civilian's house. Said it was an accident. That they were chasing a hog."

"Who just happened to run inside somebody's house?"

"That's the story."

"But you're not buying it."

"Hell, no. They were chasing someone they thought was trespassing on their still site."

"Those boys don't have a still," Gator said with way

too much conviction. But then that's why Hunter had sought him out. The man knew everything that went on in the county and beyond when it came to moonshine. "Hell, they can barely wipe their own asses without help. They're not smart enough to run their own operation."

"That's what I thought, but I have an eyewitness who puts them at the site."

"This eyewitness wouldn't happen to be the hog they were chasing, now would it?"

"Maybe."

"And you wouldn't happen to be this hog, now would you?"

"I plead the fifth."

"I see." Gator nodded. "So when do you think those morons started operating a still?"

"That's what I want to know."

"Don't look at me. I have a set clientele with a much higher IQ."

"You also have eyes in the back of your head. Nothing moves around here without you knowing it. If they're producing, they're selling, or they soon will be. I need to know if you've heard anything about anyone new trying to move some product."

"There are only a select few guys producing right now and I know for a fact that none of them would hire Cole or Monty, let alone both." His pool partner walked up and Gator motioned to his next shot. Leaning over, he jabbed the stick forward. Balls clacked and a solid slid into the right pocket.

His partner downed half his beer and looked as if he was trying not to cry.

"They're not smart enough to be doing this on their

own," Hunter said, his voice a notch lower as he focused on Gator who stepped back to let the other man take a shot. "And if none of the usuals will hire them, there must be a new guy in town."

"You really think so?"

"An experienced new guy. The setup is top notch. It's definitely somebody who's been in the game for a while."

"And you want me to ask around and see if I can find out a name?"

"You're smarter than you look."

Gator grinned before the expression flatlined. "I can get into serious trouble with my supplier if they know I'm feeding you information. They don't like snitches."

"You'll be snitching on the competition. I doubt they'd have a problem with that."

"You don't know these guys."

"Maybe they're not the ones with the problem. Maybe you are." His gaze narrowed ever so slightly as he eyed the other man. "Maybe you know exactly who I'm talking about but you're protecting them because you're working for them. If there's a new seller in town, they're going to need a channel of distribution. That means you."

But Gator wouldn't do that. He kept his operation beyond the county limits. Even more, he kept his word. A promise that he'd given a long time ago when they'd been running buddies instead of on opposite sides of the law. Hunter had done him a favor, and Gator had never forgotten it.

He owed Hunter and that meant he wouldn't screw

him over. Even more, Gator Hallsey didn't want to end up behind bars and he knew if he crossed the line into Hunter's county, he would find himself in just such a situation.

Old friendships aside, Hunter had a job to do and Gator damn well knew that.

The bootlegger grabbed the bottle of Fireball and took a long pull. "I'll let you know if I hear anything," he said when he finally came up for air. He held out the bottle to Hunter.

"That's all I'm asking." The wild, wicked scent teased his nostrils, tempting and luring him the way the scent of Jenna's perfume had done earlier that evening. This time, however, he managed to resist.

Those days were long gone, he reminded himself. Even if he had fallen off the wagon for those few seconds earlier tonight.

It was understandable.

We're talking Jenna Tucker.

Hot, sexy, irresistible. She was the most potent temptation and he'd been playing the good guy far too long. It made sense he'd slip up and lose his common sense. Once.

But not twice.

He didn't chase after women like Jenna anymore. He stuck to the mild-mannered types like Bobby's Kaitlyn. She was perfect for him now. He could keep company with her. Go on a few dates. Steal a few kisses. And maybe later they could move on to more. He was through with one-night stands with hot women who didn't make a lasting imprint on his brain.

Women with long blond hair and luscious breasts and bright green eyes. Women who tasted like sweet sorbet and decadent excitement.

His heart kicked up a notch and his throat went dry as he remembered.

And that was the trouble in a nutshell.

He couldn't forget.

Not tonight.

Not his own past.

Deep in his gut, in the dead of night, he remembered what it felt like to live for the moment, to feel the rush of excitement, to walk on the wild side. It felt good—so fucking *good*—and he couldn't help but want to feel that way again.

Just once.

Not that he was acting on that want.

He swallowed and stiffened, his muscles pulling tight along with his determination.

Yep, he was done kissing Miss Jenna Tucker. Done with his wild past. Done with acting on his impulses.

Finished. *Through*.

No matter how much he suddenly wished otherwise.

CHAPTER 12

She really needed to call it a night.

That's what Jenna told herself as she closed a box and slid it to the side to carry down later. It was almost four in the morning and she had to be at the high school Ag barn at eight A.M. sharp to look over the kids' animals. One of the lambs had caught a bad cold and Mr. Sheffield was eager to make sure nothing spread to the others. He wouldn't be happy if she strolled in late.

Late?

Like that would condemn her.

She'd already made the top spot on the Ag teacher's list of Most Hated Students of All Time. Back when he'd just been starting out at Rebel High School and she'd been a student. She'd snuck into the barn to play with the pigs without his permission and, inadvertently, let them all out. They'd rushed the football field and knocked over the top wide receiver. He'd fractured his wrist and been benched for six weeks. As a result, the team had failed to make the playoffs for the first time in ten years.

Needless to say, she'd been the most hated sophomore in town.

Except by Mr. Wide Receiver himself. While a top

prospect on the field, he'd been from the wrong side of the tracks. He'd ridden a motorcycle and worn a leather jacket, and she'd been helpless to resist the whole bad-ass vibe. She'd spent more than one Friday night nursing him back to health and feeding her reputation.

Not that she'd cared one lick what anyone had said about her.

Not then, she reminded herself.

But she cared now, which was why she was going through the attic instead of heading downstairs to bed. Three Little Higgs would be ready to demolish the house down to its foundation in just over a week and she needed everything sorted and out by then.

She dusted off the last small trunk and pressed the latch. Metal clicked and the lid popped open with a desperate groan. The stench of mothballs filled her nostrils and left a stale taste in her mouth.

She spent the next few minutes digging through the folded clothes, everything from a few slips and several pairs of nylon stockings, to a flower-print dress with boxy shoulders. A pair of black patent leather lace-up shoes sat near the bottom of the trunk, next to a faded pair of short pink gloves.

She dug into the small pouches on either side and came up with a handful of lipsticks and an old-fashioned bottle of perfume. She ran her fingers over the faded Bellodgia label and took a sniff of the spritzer.

O-kay, so mothballs weren't the only thing stinking up the inside of the case.

Setting the bottle off to the side with the rest of the items she'd trashed, she reached into the pocket that lined the lid and retrieved a stack of mail that had been rubber-banded together.

She went to drop the stack into her trash pile when something odd caught her eye. None of the letters were addressed. No recipient. No sender. Just a pile of pink envelopes that had been carefully stamped.

Pulling off the rubber band, she riffled through the stack.

She pulled open the first envelope and slid the paper from inside. Unfolding the delicate parchment, she stared at the neat script and felt a wave of nostalgia roll over her.

It had been ages since she'd seen a handwritten letter. Not since she'd unearthed the Dear Santa letters after her mother's death. The woman had saved all of the scribbled, misspelled concoctions that her daughters had painstakingly written and addressed to the Big Man up North.

With the convenience of computers and cell phones, people rarely wrote letters to each other. Like most folks, if Jenna couldn't text or e-mail, she didn't bother. As far as keeping up with friends, that's what Facebook and Instagram were for.

But this was from a far different time.

December 21, 1941 to be exact.

She had the same niggle of guilt that she'd felt when she'd stolen Callie's diary and read it from cover to cover, but it wasn't enough to deter her from what she was about to do.

She scooted back and settled against a nearby wall, her legs stretched out in front of her, and started to read.

My dearest P.J.,

I am truly sorry about what happened on Friday. I wanted to tell you that in person, but my father would not let me out of the house once he dragged me inside. He thinks if he locks me up that it will change things. That I will stop feeling the way I do. He does not know me or the depths of what I feel. He can keep me prisoner, but he cannot make me forget the love of my life. Never. Not even if he tries to beat it out of me. He won't. At least, that's what Mama says. But what does she know? I'm guilty of the ultimate betrayal as far as he's concerned. I've turned him against his best friend. I'm the enemy now. Waking up to the sharp strap of his belt would not surprise me one bit. In fact, it would be welcome to disrupt the silence that fills this room. Even Mama only stays for a few minutes when she brings me my meals. And while she at least talks to me, she never speaks of what happened. Of what is happening. All she talks about is what Rebecca Peabody was wearing at the market or the horrible gloves that Maureen Shay was wearing at church. She won't speak of the Tuckers anymore and she says I shouldn't either. She hates them now, just like my father. I cannot begin to tell you how terrible I feel about that. I have ruined everything for you and your family. All I can do is hope now that you can find it in your heart to forgive me one day.

Begging your forgiveness once again and always,

Clara Bell Sawyer

Jenna stared at the signature scribbled across the bottom and her stomach hollowed out. Shock bolted through her.

What was Clara Sawyer's trunk doing in James Harlin Tucker's attic?

Had he picked it up at a rummage sale? Won it in a game of poker? Found it abandoned on the side of the road?

A dozen possibilities swam in her head. All plausible.

At the same time, she had the gut feeling there was more to it. More to the letters.

More to the riff that had divided an entire town.

Her gaze went to the signature again and a certain tall, dark sheriff pushed into her head. Clara Bell wasn't just a Sawyer. She was Hunter's great-grandmother.

The notion stirred her memories and her mouth tingled.

So much for a distraction.

She refolded the letter, rebanded it with the rest of the stack, and closed the trunk. Pulling the cord on the overhanging bulb, she headed for the ladder leading down to the first-floor landing. A few minutes later, she dropped the stack of letters on her nightstand and headed for the bathroom. If she had any hope of getting to sleep, she needed to wash Hunter off her skin and out of her head. That meant lots of cold water and even more prayer.

Unfortunately, it was springtime in Texas. That meant heat, heat, and more heat as the days chugged their way toward a blistering summer. The water would be tepid at best. Even worse, Jenna had never put much weight in talking to The Man upstairs. Sure, she knew how to pray. She just wasn't convinced anyone was listening.

A doubt that was confirmed when she finally climbed between the sheets, Jez curled up at her back, and closed her eyes. Hunter's image came to her then to tease and tantalize and remind her of just what she was missing in her newfound walk down the straight and narrow.

So much for divine intervention.

CHAPTER 13

It was much too early in the morning for this.

Jenna stared at the mangled hem of her favorite T-shirt before shifting her attention to the culprit who'd just chewed it up while she'd been bent over, assessing a large scrape on his right shoulder.

Taz was a 160-pound medium wool cross sheep who'd gotten caught on a sharp edge of a fence at the Rebel High School Agriculture barn.

He was also a hungry 160-pound medium wool cross who'd decided to gnaw on the edge of her Texas Rebel Radio T-shirt. She snatched the large piece of material still in his mouth and gave him a stern look.

"Bad Taz," she murmured, reaching behind her into her bag for some antibiotic ointment. She fixed him up and then prepared a tetanus shot.

"There you go," she told Monica Gray, a high school sophomore and the worried owner.

"You're sure he's going to be okay? Because I've got my first prospect show in Medina County in three weeks and I need him in perfect condition."

Taz ducked his head, caught more of her hem, and *rippp* . . .

She drew in a deep, steady breath to calm her pounding heart and quell the sudden urge to yank a little of Taz's fluffy white fur in retaliation.

Not that she would, but a girl could dream, right?

Besides, if she ever were going to contemplate a little vengeance, it would be with the hellion sheep that had been giving her trouble since she'd first set eyes on him back in May. He'd chewed up the edge of her favorite pair of Sperry's. While they were on her feet.

He'd almost taken off a toe as she'd wrestled him off, and he'd been even smaller back then.

Now . . . He'd grown so fast. She knew the pair of Old Gringo boots she'd stuffed her feet into that morning didn't stand a chance if she didn't get the hell out of Dodge.

"He'll be ready to go for the show." She packed up her case and sidestepped Taz, who dipped a head and tried to catch the dusty tip of one leather boot. "Just keep it clean for the next few days and you're good to go. Speaking of going, I need to head to the office—"

"So soon?" The question came from the short blond woman who walked up to the pen. "I was hoping you could check Ryan Lawson's pig first. He's been sneezing and we think he's got a cold." She wore a teal T-shirt that read 100% COWGIRL, worn jeans, and a pair of teal cowboy boots. When she noted Jenna's questioning look, she added, "Kimberly Bowman. I'm filling in for Mr. Sheffield. He had a heart attack a few weeks ago and he's on indefinite leave."

Which explained why Jenna had been called out to the school with no special request—namely *send anyone but that Tucker*—listed in the visitation notes.

Jenna's brow wrinkled as she did a mental search. "Do I know you?"

"No, but I know you. I knew your sister Callie. Not that we were friends or anything." The woman shrugged. "She was a few years behind me in school. When I graduated, I left for College Station."

"Texas A & M?" The teacher nodded and Jenna added, "Me, too."

"Gig 'em Aggies," Kim said before adding, "After that, I moved to Austin. I had a position at Lake Travis High School for the past ten years, but then my mother passed away. She lived just outside the city limits on a small spread a stone's throw north."

Recognition hit as Jenna remembered the small obituary listed in the bottom left-hand corner of the *Rebel Gazette* opposite the livestock sales page. "Emily Sawyer?"

She nodded. "That was her married name. Then it was Thomas. Then Bowman. Then Cleeves. When she finally passed on she was Emily Harold."

"I'm sorry for your loss."

She nodded. "Thanks." She pulled a pair of work gloves from her back pocket. "So what about Tiny? Do you have time to take a look?"

She nodded and spent the next hour wrestling with the biggest pig she'd ever seen. Tiny was at least one hundred and fifty pounds and not that keen on getting his temperature taken. By the time she managed to assess him, her shirt wasn't just chewed up, it was totally screwed. The sleeve was ripped. The front was covered in mud. And Jenna herself hadn't fared much better.

"I'm really sorry," Kim said, handing her some paper

towels to wipe her face. "He's really particular about who he lets get near him."

"Most animals are." She wiped the mud off her cheek. At least she thought it was mud. A deep breath, and she grimaced. Okay, so it wasn't entirely mud.

No wonder she'd done her specialty in equine science instead of livestock. A horse was so much easier to deal with.

That, and she just liked horses.

That's what had hurt so much about not being assigned to the Sawyer Bend Horse Farm. She'd wanted that assignment because she loved horses. She loved working with them and riding and training.

All the more reason to buck up and finish what she'd started. She needed a complete makeover, from her house to her reputation, and she wasn't stopping until she'd managed to change an entire town's attitude toward wild child Jenna Tucker.

That meant no more kissing Hunter DeMassi.

Her mouth tingled at the memory. A crazy reaction because it had been hours. Plenty of time for the ten seconds of *Oh, baby* to fade into nothing.

If Hunter had been like all the other Chucks and Kevins she'd dated over the past year. Nice guys, but forgettable.

Nice or not, she wasn't forgetting this time and that made her even more irritated than not-so-tiny Tiny wrestling her into a pile of muck.

The truth followed her back to the clinic, niggling at her as she tried to focus on her work.

"So I told her, nobody in their right mind uses one stick of butter in a pie crust," Bonnie Crenshaw was telling

Miss Ann when Jenna walked into the clinic. "Any cook worth her salt knows it's two. Maybe even three."

Miss Ann nodded her agreement as she finished running Bonnie's credit card for the chocolate-brown toy poodle attached to a hot pink leash. "Why does Alma want to make a pie crust anyhow? The woman can't cook to save her life. Why start with a pie?"

"It's for her neighbor. Everybody knows that pie is Gerald Sawyer's favorite and since he's on that feeding tube, she figured she'd drop it off for poor Lorelei to stick in a blender. I still can't believe that Haywood blew half his jaw off."

"I heard it was his foot?"

"I don't know about a foot, but I heard from Maureen Samuel who heard from Shaylene Sawyer who said that her niece tended him at Rebel Memorial Hospital. Said they almost had to life flight him to Austin. But then his brother came in and gave a bunch of blood so they were able to deal with it all right there. He'll have to find a good plastic surgeon, though, but that'll be later after he's out of the woods."

"But I thought he just went to the local Urgent Care?"

"No Urgent Care can do a jaw reconstruction. Why, Haywood blew it clean off." Bonnie shook her head. "His left ear, too. Why, it'll be a miracle if the man can ever wear a pair of dentures again. They have to have the bone intact to hold the screws, you know. Why, Lorelei can kiss good-bye her yearly Christmas picture."

"Unless Gerald wants to dress up like Santa," Miss Ann offered. "I bet that white beard would hide the problem."

"Maybe so, but you got to have two good ears to hold

the ones with the elastic hoops. That, or a decent jaw-line for some temporary glue. Gerald ain't got neither now." She made a *tsk tsk* sound. "Damn that Haywood Tucker—"

The swear ended in a loud cough as Miss Ann caught sight of Jenna and both women stiffened.

"Oh, hey there, Doc," Bonnie said, making a show of shoving her credit card into her wallet. She signed the credit card receipt next and handed it back over to Ann. "Just getting Lolly her rabies shot," she blurted as if she were a toddler with her hand caught in the cookie jar. "Gotta run." She snatched up the dog and headed for the door. "Y'all take care now."

"Anybody waiting?" Jenna asked.

Miss Ann handed over a file folder. "Warren Burger brought in his Doberman." She motioned to the closed door. "Big Boy's not feeling too good. Warren said he got into the Metamucil. He's been puking and shitting for the past hour."

"Where's Doc Morris?"

"Still at lunch. I was going to call him, but here you are." She wrinkled her nose. "That, and he's got a meet-ing this afternoon and, well, you already smell pretty bad. No need to get his lab coat dirty when you're al-ready neck deep in it." The old woman smiled then, a slight gleam in her eyes as if she expected Jenna to say something.

"I had a run-in with a pig named Tiny," she managed. And that was it. No insult telling Miss Anne that smell-ing like Aqua Net and mothballs wasn't much better than reeking of Tiny. No jibe that Ann was practically an expert on the smell because she was full of it, herself.

Jenna drew a deep breath and fought to calm her prickly nerves. She was better than childish insults.

She was different now.

At that moment her cell phone rang. She glanced at the display and noted the now familiar Unavailable. She ignored the urge to let it go to voice mail. She had to nip this in the bud. Right now.

"Chuck?"

"Jenna? Thank God you answered. I was starting to think you're avoiding me."

"I'm working."

"I know. I'm sitting out front."

She twisted, her gaze going to the wall of windows that lined the front and the man parked near the curb across the street. "Are you following me?"

"I prefer to think of it as looking out for you."

"I don't need you to look out for me. There's nothing between us, Chuck. You're not the guy for me." She hit the End button before he could give her at least a dozen reasons why she was wrong.

"New boyfriend?"

"Actually, he's not my boyfriend." She ignored the urge to duck behind the desk and hide from his line of sight. No more running or avoiding the inevitable just to spare his feelings. She was giving it to him straight. "I don't have a boyfriend. I don't want a boyfriend."

"Of course not. A girl like you likes to keep her options open."

"A girl like me likes to work." Another deep breath and she fought to keep from grimacing.

Gathering her resolve, she steeled herself and headed for the closed door.

CHAPTER 14

He wasn't kissing her again.

That's what Hunter told himself the next day while he met with the mayor to go over security for the upcoming jalapeño festival scheduled for the following month. After that he handled a missing persons call when Walt Johnson lost his way home from the Piggly Wiggly thanks to his Alzheimer's. And then he went over the pics from his surveillance of Cole and Monty's still site.

Not that it was theirs. Gator was right. The Mayweather boys weren't smart enough for such a setup.

But it belonged to someone and Hunter meant to find out who.

Tonight.

After he checked on Jenna and dropped off the door he'd promised her.

Construction or not, he'd given his word and he meant to follow through.

Keeping his promise. That's what he was doing. He was looking in on her. Alleviating his worry for her safety because he'd put her in the line of fire in the first place. And replacing her door. Then he was gone. No packing up boxes or staying even a moment longer than necessary.

In and out.

The thought struck and just like that, he saw Jenna's naked body beneath him, her silky legs wrapped around his waist, her lips eating at his as his body plunged deep into hers . . .

Forget in and out.

He was stopping by and then moving on. One quick stop. Fast.

And if she tried to kiss him?

He ignored the question, along with the rush of excitement that it stirred, and hardened his resolve. He drew an easy breath as he slid the photos into an envelope and picked up a phone call that beeped on his desk.

"Sheriff DeMassi. How can I help you?"

"You can bring me an extra-large vanilla-bean Frappuccino from the new Starbucks, a slice of lemon loaf, and my shotgun."

"Hey, Mimi." Hunter slid the envelope into his bottom desk drawer. "First off, you know you can't have an extra-large vanilla-bean Frappuccino or a slice of lemon loaf because of your diabetes."

"What about the shotgun?"

"That would be a no."

"Just because I have cataracts—"

"It's not because of the cataracts, though you really ought to reconsider what the doctor said and look into the surgery. It's because the Rebel Royal Arms doesn't allow weapons of any kind. That's why they confiscated those nunchucks."

"They weren't nunchucks. They were Chubby Chucks.

I got them off QVC during their burn your way to a better bod week. I inherited your great, great, great-grandmother's flabby arms and now I can't even think about wearing a sleeveless shirt. A few moves with those babies every day and I would have been in a tank top in no time."

"You don't wear tank tops."

"Yeah, well, maybe I would if I had my nunchucks."

"You mean Chubby Chucks?"

"Whatever. If you can't bring my shotgun, then at least bring me a pellet gun. Even a water gun will do. Just so long as it looks real. Stella Blankenship is creeping on Paul Parker and I need to put a stop to it."

"Why don't you just talk to her?"

"It won't do any good. See, Paul Parker is the only eighty-eight-year-old male in here with all his teeth. He's a hot commodity. Even more so because he can't see two licks in front of his face on account of his own cataracts. As long as you smell good and talk real sweet, you're gold."

"So talk sweet."

"Can't you at least bring me a nightstick or something? A slingshot, even. I'm desperate." The pleading in her voice tugged at something inside of him and a memory stirred.

Of a sullen thirteen-year-old boy pleading for the first piece of apple pie.

She'd always come through for him every Sunday after the pot roast and potatoes. He'd follow her into the kitchen after listening to a full hour of his father gushing over how well his younger brother had thrown the football in the last peewee game, or how he'd won the fifth grade spelling bee. His brother had deserved the first slice of pie. Hell, Travis had deserved the whole damned thing, but his Mimi had always given Hunter the first.

As if he deserved it.

He hadn't. Not back then, and certainly not now. He struggled every day to keep himself walking the straight and narrow. To do the right thing instead of what he wanted to do.

But his Mimi had loved him before he'd straightened up his act. And she would love him even if he let it all go to shit.

That's what he told himself.

He just wasn't in any hurry to find out. Everyone in his life had turned on him. His mother. His father. Travis had died and they'd all blamed Hunter. Travis was good. Kind. Respectable. He hadn't deserved to die.

But Hunter . . .

He'd never been good or kind or even close to respectable. He should have been the one to bite the dust, not their precious Travis.

That's what they thought.

And while Hunter hated to admit it, he knew they were right.

They resented the fact that he'd lived while their youngest had died. They resented him.

And he couldn't blame them, because he shared that resentment.

"You're a good boy," Mimi had told him too many times to count. Even when he hadn't felt so good. *"You're meant for something else, that's all. We're not all perfect. Lord knows, most of us are far from it. You do the*

*best you can with what you're dealt. The best you can
do is take the lemons and make the best danged lemonade you can."*

And that's what he'd done.

He'd taken a volatile personality and a mean temper
and a bad-ass reputation and turned all three in his favor.
While most didn't want to go up against him in a fight,
everybody wanted him backing them up in one.

They wanted him fighting the bad guys so they didn't
have to.

A fight . . . Now that's what he needed to relieve the
tension knotting his muscles tight.

The thought struck, but he sucker-punched it right
back out of his brain.

"What about that slingshot?" Mimi's voice drew him
back to the present.

"I'll see what I can do."

"Good. Now get back to work and don't forget to
come and see me tomorrow."

As if he ever would. She was the one person who
hadn't given up on him, and he had no intention of giving up on her. His grandparents had passed on years ago,
his granddad from heart disease and his grandmother
from cancer. His mother and father had retired to Port
Aransas, partly because his dad liked fishing, but mostly
because Rebel and everyone in it reminded them of the
son they'd lost. And they hadn't been back since.

Not when Hunter had been sworn in. Or when Mimi
had moved into the Royal Rebel Arms. Being away was
easier for them.

And hard for his great-grandmother because she had
no one now.

He slid the phone into place, finished up the paperwork on his desk before pushing to his feet. He grabbed his cell phone and keys and headed for the rear parking lot.

He needed a distraction from his thoughts and the anxiety pushing and pulling inside of him. An urge that made him want to hit the nearest rodeo arena and see if he could still ride a wild bronc the way he used to.

He couldn't. He already knew that. He'd ridden without a care in the world back in the day because he hadn't had a care in the world. He'd been wild back then. Dangerous. *Free*.

Tamping down on the rush of adrenaline that pumped through him, he drew a deep, calming breath and focused on the first name blazing on his phone courtesy of one Gator Hallsey.

He needed to spend some energy and there was no better way to do it than chasing down bad guys.

By the time five o'clock rolled around, Jenna had had her fill of pig shit, dog barf, and a hamster named Chloe who took a nice little chunk out of her thumb. She was ready to head home, straight into a hot shower.

Or rather, a lukewarm shower because, like everything else at the Tucker spread, her hot water heater was on its last legs.

All the more reason to rejoice when she pulled down the gravel drive to find a giant yellow bulldozer scooping up the last remains of the small barn that had sat on the far corner of her property.

Her stomach hollowed out and she reached inside the

bakery bag she'd picked up at Brandy's. Two cupcakes later and she still hadn't managed to plug the hole in her stomach.

"I told you we'd get the entire thing torn down in one day," Brody Higgs told her when she finally worked up her nerve to exit her vehicle. He tipped back the edge of his white hard hat and eyed the stack of debris where the small building had once been. "Of course, we'll need one more day for cleanup and then the boys will start framing the new building." He checked off a line on his clipboard before turning his attention to the house. "We might even get to this dwelling a few days ahead of schedule."

"That's great," she said after swallowing a mouthful. Her throat closed around a few crumbs and she cleared her suddenly dry throat. "The sooner, the better obviously."

"So you'll be ready?" He eyed her. "Can't have anything left inside."

"I'll be ready," she assured him. One last look at the pile of rubble and she blinked against a sudden burning behind her eyes.

A crazy reaction because she'd never liked that barn. It had housed all the leftover crap that James Harlin hadn't managed to squeeze into the house. From empty Country Crock butter containers, to a box of old Happy Meal toys he'd picked up going through the drive-thru at the local McDonald's every Friday. Like clockwork, he'd bought Jenna a Happy Meal and one for himself each week when she'd been in the sixth grade. That had been the first year that both Callie and Brandy had worked after school and so her care had fallen to James Harlin who'd rolled up in his old pickup every day like clockwork.

Most days, she reminded herself. There had been a few times he'd been passed out and she'd had to walk home.

But never on a Friday.

He'd always managed to show up with McDonald's on the line.

She'd kept her toy, but he'd boxed his up because "a fella never knows when he'll need a Superman bobble-head," or so he'd told her. "Or a miniature American Girl doll or a Pokemon figurine."

Grandkids.

That's why he'd stashed the toys. Because despite all James Harlin's meanness, he'd expected great-grandkids one day and he'd meant to be ready for them the way he hadn't been ready for his own grandkids.

At least that's what Jenna had told herself.

Truth be told he was probably just a selfish bastard who didn't want anyone touching his stuff. That's what Callie had always said and she was usually right.

Still . . .

Jenna stared into the box of unopened Happy Meal toys, from the My Little Pony miniatures to the Hot Wheels cars, before closing the cardboard and taping the lid shut. There was a Sunday school class full of kids down at the local First Presbyterian Church who were going to be very happy.

A fact that should make her very happy.

She knew that, but damned if she could muster up the emotion. Instead, she ate a third cupcake before heading for her bedroom to take a shower and wash off what remained of Tiny the pig and Big Boy the Doberman.

Afternoon sunlight streamed through the sheer pink eyelet curtains covering the bedroom windows, bathing the room in a glow that would have been warm if she'd been any other place but Texas.

Instead it was hot.

Sweltering.

She ended up taking a cold shower before doctoring her thumb with some Neosporin and a Band-Aid. Pulling on a Rebel County Rodeo Finals T-shirt and a pair of shorts, she retrieved a glass of iced tea from the kitchen. Returning to her bedroom, she sank down on the edge of her bed, Jez beside her, and eyed the letters.

She really should hand them over to Hunter. They had his great-grandmother's name on them, after all.

At the same time, she had a crapload of boxes to pack up if she meant to be ready a few days before the projected demolition date for the house. That meant she wasn't going anywhere with the letters until she'd finished the house.

That, and she'd found them in *her* house. Which meant that somehow they were connected to the Tuckers.

Written, as a matter of fact, to one Tucker in particular.

Because Clara Bell had loved this particular Tucker, and that love had torn the two families apart?

Jenna was starting to think so, but there was only one way to be sure.

She pulled the next letter free from the stack and unfolded the worn paper. Scooting back up, she rested her back against the headboard, sipped her iced tea and started to read.

My dearest P.J.,

It feels like forever since I have picked up my pen to write to you. In truth, it has been only one month, but one of the longest of my life. Things are getting worse since everyone found out the truth. Of course, by everyone I mean my folks. The world is still ignorant of what happened. They know only that my father hates your father. A thief. That's what some folks are calling your father. At least that's what my older sisters tell me. They go out to ice cream socials and Sunday barbecues while I bide my time inside a locked room. They feed me the gossip through a closed door. The lock opens only for my parents who look at me so differently than they once did. As if I'm the traitor, when in all honesty, they are the ones who betrayed me. They keep pushing and pushing for me to be someone I'm not. For me to do what they want. To say what they want. To be what they want. They thought I was perfect, but now they know that was just an illusion. They see that I have my own ideas. I still do even though it gets harder and harder with each day that passes to remember as much. To remember that I love working in the garden and riding my horse and tending to the animals, just like you. But I'm supposed to admire music and art and theater, like all proper young ladies. Like my sisters. My mother. She's a cut above the women in this godforsaken town. That's why my father traveled all the way to Chicago to marry her. He wanted a real lady. He wants me to be a real lady, too. But I'm not. I will never be, and everyone will know it soon enough now that I have the proof of my indiscretion growing inside me.

I care not, of course, and that only makes my father more determined to shut me off from everything that I do care about. He sold my horse yesterday and stomped the baby tomatoes I was growing out near the barn. A real lady doesn't ride a wildling Paint that's too stubborn for its own good. A real lady doesn't get her hands dirty. He wants to smother the spirit inside of me, but I will not let him. I will never reject this child. I will keep it safe just as I will continue to love the father until my last dying breath. Even if my own father sends me back to Chicago to be with my aunt. I swear to you now that distance will not weaken what I feel.

Still begging your forgiveness,
Clara Bell Sawyer

Forget a mere forbidden love. There'd been much more at stake when the families had split.

The truth echoed as Jenna re-read the words a second time and then a third.

Like everyone else in town, Jenna had heard the rumors about what had caused the rift between Archibald Tucker and Elijah G. Sawyer. Elijah had stolen from Archibald. Archibald had swindled Elijah. Elijah had slept with Archibald's woman. Archibald had given it to Elijah's wife. The rumors had been plenty, most of them centering around an illicit affair or money, or both, but no one had ever really known the truth except the two men directly involved.

Until now.

Clara Bell Sawyer had gotten pregnant and while the name P.J. didn't ring a bell in Jenna's memory, she knew by Clara's own words in the first letter that he was a hated Tucker.

More than an affair, a *baby* had divided the families.

A secret baby that was both Tucker and Sawyer.

The notion was the stuff of one of those 80's prime-time soap operas trending on Netflix, like *Dallas* or *Falcon Crest*. Dramas rich in big hair, massive shoulder pads and jaw-dropping twists and turns.

Dozens of questions rolled around in her head, but she didn't have to wait for the next season to get some answers. Instead she pulled the next letter free.

She was just about to unfold the delicate paper when she glanced at her blinking phone, noted Chuck's now familiar Unavailable, and let it go to voice mail. How many times did she have to explain that she wasn't interested?

As many as it took, her conscience told her.

Be nice. Let him down easy. Be persistent. Kind.

But not at this moment. She'd had hell today and she needed an escape.

One that didn't involve Hunter DeMassi's lips.

Ignoring the sudden memory that rushed at her, she took a long gulp of the iced tea. And then she snuggled down, shifted her attention to letter number three, and started to read.

CHAPTER 15

"You done for the day, Sheriff?" Marge's voice crack-led over the radio when Hunter climbed back into his truck after two hours spent tracking down a man by the name of Will Canyon.

Turned out Will wasn't so hard to find, after all. He'd been playing dominos at the VFW Hall along with a handful of old men and Linda Mae, Rebel's one and only female mechanic and ex-Navy pilot. A piece of in-formation Hunter would have welcomed before he'd driven clear across the county only to discover that the address on file belonged to the man's son, Will Jr.

"It's Tuesday. That means Dad is at the Rebel VFW Hall," forty-two-year-old Will Jr. had told Hunter. "He plays dominoes every Tuesday with Shorty Tucker and then stays for supper on account of it's meatloaf night for the veterans."

Not that Will Sr., at age sixty-three had ended up be-ing the owner of the still. Sure, he fit the bill. His cata-racts were so bad that it stood to reason he might hire the Mayweather boys since he couldn't very well see how ill equipped they were to handle things. But, as it turns out, the man had little knowledge of moonshine, evident in those few moments that Hunter had been watching while the man was unaware. Will Sr. had taken a sip that Linda had offered him, only to spew out the mouthful smack-dab into Shorty Tucker's face.

"Dagnabbit," Shorty had muttered. "You just ruined my new shirt."

"It ain't my fault," Will Sr. had sputtered. "It's this stuff. Just what the hell *is* this?"

And if he had to ask, he certainly wasn't Hunter's guy.

"I didn't say it was him," Gator told Hunter when he punched in the bootlegger's cell number. "I just said that one of my contacts heard his name tossed around."

"Your contact is full of shit. I even checked out the son. His record's clean. Not even a traffic violation."

"Maybe he's just smart."

"And maybe your contacts are for shit."

"That's possible, too, but they're all I've got right now. Check out the other names that were given to me and see if anything shakes out."

Two more dead-end possibilities and Hunter was even more anxious than when he'd started out a few hours ago.

"Sheriff? You done?" Marge asked again.

But Hunter was never done. The job pulled at him twenty-four/seven.

Thankfully, he reminded himself. He didn't need the downtime to sit around and think.

Regret.

He stiffened against the notion. "I still need to follow up on a few things. I'll be on my radio. Call if you need me."

A few minutes later, he climbed into the beige SUV, tugged at the top button on his shirt, and drew a deep breath. While he'd grown accustomed to the uniform, it still bothered him every once in a while. Especially when the weather started heating up and . . . there.

He popped the last button and slid off the shirt until he wore only the white T-shirt beneath. Tossing the stifling beige to the seat, he keyed the ignition and headed for the run-down farmhouse that sat outside of town.

He couldn't very well hit the local honky-tonk and pick a fight to burn off some steam. Or pick out a woman to burn up the sheets. He had a reputation to uphold, after all.

But kissing Jenna Tucker again in the privacy of her own home? Away from prying eyes and the gossips who had fed off his antics so long ago?

While it wasn't the best choice, suddenly it seemed like the only one if he meant to hold onto his sanity and his control for the time being. Forget simply delivering a door and doing his civic duty. Another kiss might make him forget the first and that would be a good thing, right?

Damn straight it would.

Damn *straight*.

He was kissing her again.

There'd been no casual conversation. No easing into the moment. Just a knock on the door and bam, he was here. Now.

Kissing her.

Uh-oh.

Hunter's strong, purposeful mouth moved over hers

as he backed her into the hallway and kicked the front door shut with his boot. His tongue swept her bottom lip, licking and nibbling and coaxing and . . .

Wait a second. Wait just a freakin' *second*. This shouldn't be happening. Not here. Not with him. Especially not him.

Just as the denial registered in her shocked brain, he deepened the kiss.

His tongue pushed inside, to tease and taunt and tangle with hers. All reasoning faded into a whirlwind of hunger that swirled through her like a tornado ripping through West Texas. Her heart started to thunder. Her adrenaline started to pump. Her nerves started to spin.

She trembled and her stomach hollowed out.

Before she could stop herself, she leaned into him, melting from the sudden rise in body temperature. Her hand slid up his chest and her fingers caught the soft hair at the nape of his neck.

His arms closed around her. Strong hands pressed against the base of her spine, drawing her closer. She met him chest for chest, hip for hip, until she felt every incredible inch of him flush against her body—the hard planes of his chest, the solid muscles of his thighs, the growing erection beneath his zipper.

Uh-oh.

The warning sounded in her head, but damned if it didn't make her that much more excited. Heat spread from her cheeks, creeping south. The slow burn traveled inch by sweet, tantalizing inch, until her nipples throbbed and wetness flooded between her thighs.

And all because of a kiss.

Because of *his* kiss.

But Hunter DeMassi wasn't wild and careless and completely inappropriate. He was the town's sheriff, for heaven's sake, and damned if she didn't want him— really want him—anyway.

It was the moment she'd been waiting for. The mild-mannered guy she'd been searching for.

That's what her head said. But her instincts told her he was far too dangerous to be the right man.

To be a good man.

The thought struck and she stiffened. Tearing her lips away, she stumbled backward.

"I . . . You . . ." She shook her head and tried to ignore the way her lips tingled. "You and I . . ." She shook her head again. "I don't think we should be doing this."

"We shouldn't." He said the words, but the strange flicker in his gaze didn't mirror the sentiment. "But I want to, anyway, and damned if I can help myself."

"But I'm not like that anymore. I don't sleep around."

"Trust me. There won't be any sleeping involved." His gaze darkened as it touched her mouth and she felt the overwhelming chemistry that pulsed between them. "Not a single second."

Oh, boy.

She forced an easy breath, wishing with all her being that her lips would stop trembling. They didn't any more than her heart slowed its frantic pace. Still, she had to get it together. To think. Talk.

Another deep breath and she gathered her resolve. "Listen, I know I might have given you the wrong impression last night," she tried again. "I shouldn't have kissed you. That was a mistake. And this is a mistake. You should go," she went on, desperate to kill the tiny hope that he would pull her close, kill her stupid resolve, and kiss her again.

Lust.

That's all this was.

That, and deprivation.

She'd been walking the straight and narrow for so long that it made sense that she would blow at the first sign of temptation.

But he shouldn't be tempting her in his beige pants and simple white T-shirt. There was nothing remotely sexy about his getup, and yet there was just something about the way his shirt clung to his broad shoulders and accented his thick biceps. A five o'clock shadow covered his jaw and his hair looked as if he'd raked a hand through it one too many times.

He didn't look nearly as put together as he usually did. Instead, he looked as if he was unraveling, shedding his buttoned-up image.

Cutting loose.

It only stood to reason that her starving hormones would shift into overdrive at the notion.

"I can't just go around hopping into bed with every man who propositions me. I mean, yes, I liked the kiss, but that's beside the point. We're all wrong for each other."

"You say that like it matters."

"It does."

A grin tugged at the corner of his sensuous lips. "I don't want to date you, Jenna." His gaze collided with hers. "I want to have sex with you."

She wasn't sure why his words sent a wave of disappointment through her. It's not like she *wanted* to date him.

She had a slew of dates behind her with guys just like him and they'd all been a waste of her time.

She needed to focus. To get back to work.

Her gaze went to the boxes stacked nearby. "This isn't right."

"Tell me about it." His deep voice drew her attention and she saw the battle in his gaze. A tug-of-war that mirrored her own. The realization sent a ripple of camaraderie through her, followed by a wave of disappointment.

"I know I'm not exactly your type," she heard herself say.

"No, you're not," he agreed much too quickly.

"If that's the case, then what's this all about?"

"It's about the fact that I can't stop thinking about you and I need to."

He was saying everything she was thinking, and damned if it didn't bother her. It was as if he stared past the excuses, straight into the heart of things.

Of her.

"I can't do this. I don't *want* to do this. I've got a lot on my plate right now and this, whatever this is, is not a good idea." At least that's what she was frantically telling herself. "You should just go." Before he could respond, she scooted past him and hauled open the front door. "Now. Please," she added, the plea little more than a desperate whisper.

He didn't look as if he meant to oblige. The seconds ticked by while a war waged inside of her between her hormones and her common sense. She wanted to grab him and never let go almost as much as she wanted to kick him out the door.

Because as much as Hunter looked and acted like the calm, reputable, tame sheriff, he still called to the bad girl inside of her. There was just something about him . . . Something wild and *un*tamed that made her want to forget her vow to walk the straight and narrow. Forget her hopes and dreams.

Herself.

"You're right," he said abruptly, as if he'd just waged his own war and reason had emerged the victor.

Damn reason.

She smothered the last thought and managed a quick "Thanks for stopping by," before closing the door behind him.

And then she headed back to the bedroom.

To the stack of letters and the blossoming story of Clara Bell and her secret baby, and the one remaining cupcake. While chocolate was a poor substitute for sex, it was all she had at the moment.

That, and the letters.

CHAPTER 16

"It's about damn time." Clara Bell Sawyer took the white bakery bag that Hunter handed her and pulled out the jumbo peanut butter cookie he'd picked up at Sweet Somethings Bakery on his way over. "What's this?" She gave the cookie a sniff. "You know I hate peanuts."

"That's because the cookie isn't for you. It's for your friend. The one interested in your fella." He winked. "I figured you could kill her with kindness."

"I'd rather do it with a slingshot." She set the bag to the side and held up her arms. "Come on and give your old Mimi some sugar. The good kind. Not this processed stuff."

He hugged the frail old woman and ignored the sudden tightening in his chest. Her hugs had always been so strong and solid, but now she was just a slip of the woman she'd once been. Her arms barely tightened and then she was shrinking away, back into the wheelchair. He noted the hollows beneath her eyes a split second before her face crinkled into a smile. "Sit down and tell me all about your week."

"You mean fill you in on all the gossip?"

She shrugged. "An old woman needs some excitement in her life."

"I take it you haven't been sweet-talking the guy with the teeth."

"Oh, I've been talking. It just turns out that he has a hearing aid which none of us knew about. He's been tuning out everyone except Louise Aldridge Tucker. Seems he's sweet on her. Can't say as I blame him. She's got all of her teeth and she can still eat a chili dog."

"Sounds like quite a catch."

"If you're into chili dogs. But it's better this way I s'pose. Now I can turn my attention to finding someone who won't aggravate my gastroenteritis every time we make out."

A grin tugged at his lips. He wanted to reach out and tell her there were plenty more fish in the sea, but she was stuck in a very small pond, so he decided to distract her instead.

That and this was his great-grandmother. The last thing he wanted was to be giving her advice on her love life.

Instead he spent the next half hour telling her about the various happenings around town, complete with Gerald and Haywood's latest disagreement and the big toe incident.

Disappointment crinkled her worn face. "Are you shitting me?"

"Jesus, Mimi." He glanced around at the old women clustered nearby, all hunched over their needlepoint. "Language."

"Trust me. There's nothing I can say that these old biddies haven't heard before even if they won't admit it.

His big toe? That's it? 'Cause Merline Evangeline said that Haywood blew Gerald's arm off and then went after him Bobbitt style with his pocketknife."

"He's still got both arms and I'm sure he and Lorelei can repopulate if the mood strikes them."

She made a *pshhh* sound. "The old fools around here. Why, none of 'em could keep a story straight if their lives depended on it."

"Hazards of a small town." He repeated Jenna's words and tried to ignore the image that rushed at him. Of Jenna arched against the wall, her lips parted and full, her breaths coming fast and furious as she stared up at him with passion-glazed eyes.

She wanted him but she didn't want to want him, and damned if that didn't bother him.

It's for the best, a voice whispered. If she hadn't put the brakes on, he might not have had the will to do it and then he'd be right where he started.

Back to making poor decisions, acting on impulse, *living* rather than thinking.

It didn't matter that she was attempting to change her image. Jenna was still every bit the bad girl he'd given up and he didn't intend to fall right back into old habits.

He'd promised himself.

He'd promised his Mimi.

"Lookee what we have here," a familiar voice sounded just as Pam Tucker Laraby walked up. She was in her midthirties with the signature Tucker blond hair and green eyes. She wore the usual pink scrubs with the familiar Royal Rebel Arms logo on the front pocket and a warm smile. A vase filled with gardenias overflowed her arms. "It's your weekly flower delivery, Miss Clara."

A smile touched his Mimi's face as she leaned forward to smell the vase full that Pam set on the table in front of her.

"I don't know what you did to make a man fall hard enough to send you flowers once a week for practically *ever*, but if you could share, I'd be eternally grateful."

"It's all in the hips," Mimi said, giving the girl a wink despite the fact that Pam was a hated Tucker.

A fact that should have dug in his Mimi's craw like it did every other person from her generation. They'd been the ones on the front lines for all the years since the feud began. The ones holding tight to the hate, perpetuating the war.

Everyone except for his Mimi.

She'd never had a bad word to say about the Tuckers. Quite the opposite, she'd always been kind and good to everyone around her, even the Tuckers.

Especially the Tuckers.

He watched as she caught Pam's hand and held tight for a second. "Put them in my room, will you, sugar?"

"Sure thing," Pam murmured before giving Hunter a nod and turning to head down the hall.

"So who's the secret admirer?" He asked the same question every week when the flowers arrived. As usual, she waved him off the way she always did.

"It's no secret. Jimmy over at the florist knows I like gardenias, that's all. He used to order extra and send them to his mother. Now that she's gone, he sends them to me. So where were we? Oh, yeah. Gerald and his missing penis."

"I already told you. Haywood didn't cut anything off."

"No, but he wanted to and that's enough to fuel the gossip here for at least another week until you get back over here to set me straight on the comings and goings of this boring-as-hell town." She grinned and a devilish light touched her eyes. "Any streakers this week?"

"That was last month and it was only because Cory Wellborn got locked out of his house while picking up the newspaper."

"I heard he mooned the paperboy."

"Not intentionally. He was picking up the sports section."

"In his birthday suit."

Hunter shrugged. "A man can do what he wants in his own house."

"Until his wife locks him out because he forgot to take out the garbage and she wants to teach him a lesson. Then it becomes your problem."

"There was no problem. He called it in himself—thankfully he'd left his cell phone in his car. He hid in the front seat until we got there with a blanket. No streaking."

"Except that Isabel Jeffries saw him from across the street and told her mother who runs the bunko table here on Wednesday nights. She told all of us and gave us quite the description. You wouldn't happen to have any pictures?" She wiggled her silver eyebrows. "You know, some leftover evidence so I can see if my mental image is close to the real thing?"

"You are ninety-two, right? Because you act like you just hit puberty." She chuckled and he added, "You ought to behave yourself."

"There's plenty of time for that when they put me in

the grave." She grabbed the bakery bag and glanced inside. "Kindness, huh?"

"I'm sure if you talk to her woman-to-woman and explain that you're interested in this Paul whatshisname, she'll respect that."

"Or she might keel over, straight into a sugar coma. She's diabetic, too, you know."

He didn't or he never would have brought her a cookie. "Maybe I ought to take that back . . ."

"Keep your paws off. I've got plans for this cookie." She stuffed it down beside her and motioned for Pam who had returned to the common area and was straightening magazines on a nearby rack. "Can you be a dear and help me back to my room?"

"I can do it—" Hunter started, but Mimi waved him silent.

"I won't have you fussing over me. I'm not an invalid. I can damn well do it myself."

Only she couldn't. He watched as she tried to undo the brakes on her chair, but her strength was failing her and it was Pam who finally hit the lever.

He noted the hollows beneath her eyes then as if she wasn't sleeping as well as she usually did and something twisted inside of him. "Hey." He caught her hand. "Are you okay?"

A strange gleam lit her gaze and she opened her mouth as if she wanted to say something, but then her lips pursed and she shook her head.

"I'm as mean as ever and twice as spry," she snapped, "and don't you forget it." He grinned then and she waved him off. "Go out and have some fun once in a while. You look old."

But she was the one looking old all of a sudden.

The image followed him out the front door of the senior living facility and stayed with him as he folded himself into his SUV and keyed the engine.

Old? Of course she was old. She was one of the town's oldest citizens, second only to Shorty Tucker who beat her out by a few weeks.

It made sense she would look her age even if he was just noticing it.

Looks aside, she was still every bit as outlandish as ever. He held tight to the thought and turned his attention to the name and address blazing on his cell phone.

The latest in a list of dead ends courtesy of Gator and his so-called contacts.

But Hunter was through chasing shadows.

He floored the gas and hit the interstate. It was time Gator gave him a viable lead.

CHAPTER 17

"What the hell are you doing way out here?" Gator stood in the doorway of the small cabin located at the dead end of a dirt road just off the main highway. Trees shrouded the entire area and crickets buzzed. It was an old hunting spot that had once belonged to Gator's grandfather.

The place had changed little in all the years since Hunter's last visit. The porch had started to sag and the beams that had once been polished to a high sheen seemed faded and worn. The paint on the small rocking chair on the porch had started to peel and cigarette butts littered the ground nearby.

He could still picture the three bootleggers—Gator Hallsey, Cooper McGraw, and Ryder Jax—gathered on the small porch, a hemi sitting in the driveway, waiting for their next delivery.

Bronc busting hadn't paid off that often for Hunter in his early days and so he'd done a few runs with the trio to supplement his income. He'd been right here the night he'd received the news about his brother. His beeper had gone off, but it hadn't been any of the shiners who used Hunter and Gator to run their product for them.

It had been his parents' number and he'd known in a heartbeat that something was very wrong. He still didn't know how his father had gotten the beeper number, except that the man had had connections in Rebel. He'd been an attorney before he'd retired and so it made sense that he'd called in a few favors to get in touch with his eldest son in the wake of tragedy.

That, or he'd known all along what Hunter had been involved in. Who he'd been running with.

Which explained why he'd been so ashamed of his son. So condemning.

At the same time, he'd been ashamed and condemning long before Hunter had taken up with Gator and his buddies. Even as a kid, Hunter had never been good enough for Jim DeMassi. He'd never made good enough grades or hung out with the right kids or helped with the collection plate at church. He'd been too busy having fun, sowing his wild oats, *living* instead of going through the motions like his parents and all of their friends.

He ignored the notion and focused on the cabin and the man who'd hauled open the door, a beer in one hand and his cell in the other.

Not that the cabin was Gator's home. Even Hunter wasn't clear exactly where the bootlegger hung his hat. The cabin was a place to crash. To wait. To exchange goods.

He glanced past Gator to the modest interior, from the small table near a stove and refrigerator, to the sofa and big-screen TV. Not a jar of shine in sight, but then Hunter hadn't expected to see anything. Gator was too careful.

"I need a real lead."

"I gave you what I had."

"You gave me shit."

"Hey, man." He shrugged, moving back to let Hunter in. "You should chill. I'm giving you everything I can. That's all I know."

"So ask around some more. I need a name."

Gator shut the door and finished a text on his phone before shifting his attention back to Hunter. "The Mayweather boys not leading you anywhere?"

The Mayweather boys hadn't left their house in the days since Hunter had dragged them in. Instead, they were holed up inside, ordering takeout and watching re-runs of *Breaking Bad*. At least according to Bobby who'd been spying on them since Hunter had let them go.

"We think whoever hired them might have fired them. They haven't returned to the still site."

"That makes sense. If this operation is top notch like you say, they were bound to wise up to those guys. They're idiots." Gator took a long swig of the beer in his hands before motioning to Hunter. "You want one?" When he shook his head, Gator sank down on the nearby sofa. "Seems to me you're pressing the wrong guy. I don't know anything, but the Mayweather boys do. You should be pressing them."

"Not yet."

"Why not?"

"Because I don't want to spook whoever owns the operation. That'll make this even more difficult. Right now, no one knows that I'm on to them. If I start pressing, any shiner worth their salt will see me coming a mile away."

"You're pressing me," Gator pointed out.

"I'm asking for a favor. There's a difference. You owe me."

"So you keep reminding me."

But Hunter didn't have to remind him. Gator would never forget that Hunter had been the one to save his younger brother from a major bust that would have ruined the kid's life. Gator's kid brother had been a star running back for one of the local high schools and well on his way to playing for a major college. He'd been offered a full ride to four of the Big 12 schools.

Kip Hallsey had had a chance at something more and Hunter had been instrumental in making sure he didn't get caught up in the raid that had sent half a dozen men to jail. Not Gator, of course. He'd been too smart. The man could smell a setup a mile away and he'd kept his distance that night. But his younger brother hadn't had the same instincts.

Hunter had been there when the shit had hit the fan and he'd taken the heat for Kip. He'd stepped up and claimed the entire case of alcohol as his own.

Hunter had sat behind bars for the thirty-eight days between arrest and trial. There'd been no one bailing him out. No one giving him a second chance. He'd escaped conviction because of a lack of evidence, not because his father had been pushing for his innocence. The man had never stood up for him. Not then.

Not now.

But he didn't need him anymore. Hunter could stand

up for himself and everyone else. He'd been doing it for two consecutive terms now.

And he was pushing for a third. One he would surely win. It was just a matter of filing the paperwork and putting his name on the ballot.

Which he had every intention of doing.

Soon.

But first he needed to check in with Bobby and make sure the Mayweather boys were still at home. Then he needed to head out to the still site and see who'd been put on guard duty.

If the Mayweathers had been fired, then someone else had been hired to take their place.

"Find me a name," he told Gator.

The man ran a hand through his hair. "I'll do my best. Now, if you know what's good for you, you'll get out of here. I'm expecting someone." When Hunter arched an eyebrow, he added, "You don't want to know, Sheriff."

"I don't know why you don't just move in with me and Tyler," Brandy told Jenna when she stopped off at the bakery to pick up more cupcakes. The place had closed a half hour ago, but Brandy was always putting in overtime to prep for the following day and so her sisters often stopped by to catch up with each other. And snag some free baked goods. "We've got an extra bedroom."

"You're newlyweds. You don't need a houseguest right now."

"You're not a houseguest. You're my sister. And you're moving in with me."

"It's only for two weeks. They're demolishing the house last and then they'll start construction right away."

"Two weeks can easily turn to three and then four. It's construction, Jenna. It's not guaranteed."

"Brody promised it wouldn't take more than two weeks. Three at the most."

"Which is exactly why you should stay with us. You haven't let me help at all with the cleanup. We lived there once, too. We all contributed to the mess."

"You've got your hands full here. I can handle the house. I'm finished with the attic and now I'm working my way through the bottom rooms."

"The entire attic?"

She nodded. "It was a bitch, but I made it. There was so much stuff. Granddad kept everything, most of which was a whole lot of nothing. But I did come across a few sentimental pieces."

Brandy arched an eyebrow. "Such as?"

"I found a trunk with a bunch of women's clothing."

"Grandma's?"

"That's what I thought at first, but it turns out the trunk belongs to someone else. Clara Bell Sawyer."

Brandy's eyebrows drew together. "What's her trunk doing in James Harlin's attic?"

"That's what I'm trying to figure out. There were letters in there, too. She never mailed them because there was no address, but they're definitely meant for someone. I think she had something going on with one of the Tuckers."

"Back then? Talk about a scandal."

"I think it was *the* scandal. I think Clara Bell had

something to do with the feud." She thought about telling Brandy about the secret baby, but she still had half the stack of letters to get through and she didn't want to say anything while there were still more questions than answers.

That, and it felt wrong somehow to talk about the letters with her sisters.

A crazy feeling because she confided everything to her sisters. But this . . .

This didn't feel right.

She shrugged. "I'm probably jumping to conclusions. It's probably nothing. I should just throw it all away and be done with it. I've still got so much stuff to get through."

"Which I would gladly help with," Brandy pushed.

"Me, too," Callie offered, coming from the back room, a pie in hand. She'd stopped in after turning in her weekly column at the newspaper. "I can box things up and take you home with me. Brett and I have plenty of room and we would love to have you." She fed the pie into a pie box that Brandy handed her.

"I can't drive all the way from Brett's ranch to the clinic every day. I'm on call most of the time. I need to be close." Jenna steeled herself against her sisters' persuasive looks and voiced her decision. "I'm staying in town at the motel."

"But—"

"Stop. I appreciate the both of you. Really I do. But I'm staying at the motel. You need your privacy," she told Brandy. "And you need it, too," she told Callie, "otherwise I'll never be an aunt."

A soft look touched her eldest sister's expression. "Actually, you might not be waiting too much longer."

The air lodged in Jenna's chest. "What exactly are you saying?"

"Nothing for certain. I'm just a few days late. It could be a false alarm." A smile touched Callie's lips. "But I have an appointment with Dr. McGhee next week just in case."

"And you're going to wait until then to find out?" Brandy screeched. "What's wrong with you? Go over to the pharmacy and get a pregnancy test."

Callie shook her head. "Brett's out of town until Friday and I want to wait for him. If there's news, I want us to find out together."

Because Callie loved Brett and he loved her. *Together*.

"I guess I can understand that," Brandy said.

Because Brandy loved Tyler and he loved her. *Together*.

Her sisters were now card-carrying members of the couple club, while Jenna stood on the outside looking in.

For the first time, the notion stirred a niggle of jealousy. A ridiculous feeling because Jenna had been in the couple club several times herself. With Chuck. And Kevin. And Marc. And Wallace. And . . . Too many men, none of whom had been the right man.

And so she was flying solo now, and happy to do it.

She *wanted* to be by herself. To prove to an entire town that she truly had changed.

Still . . . The look on Callie's face, the softness of her gaze, the happiness in her expression, made Jenna think that maybe being in love wasn't such a bad thing. With the right man.

She found herself thinking about Hunter, about the way he'd kissed her and how she really, *really* wanted him to do it again.

Because of lust, not love. She hardly knew him and he hardly knew her and hot kisses didn't make a solid foundation for any relationship.

Sure, it couldn't hurt.

But there had to be more.

As in hot sex?

The notion struck and she stiffened. She wasn't thinking about sex with Hunter. Or fantasizing about it. Or wanting it.

No.

"Do you have any blueberry pie?" Callie asked. "I could really go for some right now."

Brandy and Jenna exchanged glances. "Yep, she's pregnant, all right," Brandy said. "You hate blueberries," she pointed out to their eldest sister.

"Not really. I've only had them a few times."

"And you hated them every time."

"I think *hate* is a strong word."

"Detested them?" Jenna offered. "Because I distinctly remember you taking a bite of a scone at the last ladies' auxiliary bake sale and literally spitting it back out on the table in front of old lady Hester and Myrtle Simcox."

"It went down the wrong pipe, that's all. It was either spit it back out or have old lady Hester try to Heimlich me." She sniffed. "I definitely smell blueberries." Her eyes lit with excitement. "You just pulled some pies out of the oven, right?"

"They're tarts and you're definitely pregnant." Brandy retrieved a small box and disappeared into the back room for a full five minutes before emerging with a half-dozen tarts. Closing the box, she handed it to Callie. "Knock yourself out. And what about you?" she asked, turning to Jenna. "Any cravings?"

Just one.

Hunter's image whispered through her head and she stiffened. "Very funny." She swallowed past the sudden lump in her throat. "Just give me the cupcakes."

"Six, huh?" Brandy asked as she pulled the chocolate confections from the case and stuffed them into a pink bakery box.

Jenna thought of the kiss again and the empty house waiting for her at home and her stomach hollowed out. "Better make it a full dozen."

CHAPTER 18

Were there *any* nice, normal heterosexual men left in the world? The question echoed through Kimberly Bowman's mind early Thursday evening as she sat on the patio at The Green Bean, the one and only health food spot in Rebel. She stared across an overflowing platter of watercress and cucumber slices to the man who sat opposite her, folded into the small wrought-iron chair

Gabe Witherspoon.

He was the head of the science department at Rebel High and the latest prospect in her search for the perfect man. Kim, in her most secret, private fantasies had always envisioned a tall, dark, and handsome man with killer eyes and a sexy smile and a bit of a bad-boy streak.

And hands . . . She definitely pictured large, strong, callused hands.

A cross between Justin Timberlake and the Marlboro man.

Gabe, all five feet five inches of him, had short dishwater-brown hair, a pale complexion, and a perfectly knotted bow tie. Very un-Marlboro-esque, but then beggars couldn't be choosers.

And that's what she was at the moment, a beggar. A desperate, I need to find someone before my lady parts shrivel up and die beggar.

She glanced at the scooter parked outside near the curb and swallowed past the sudden lump in her throat.

So he wasn't the Marlboro man?

After six months of serious searching, complete with enough first dates to qualify her for some kind of desperate single woman's record, Gabe was the closest she'd come to her dream man. Hell, he was the closest she'd come to any man and so Kim wasn't going to write him off simply because he didn't measure up to her fantasy man. In fact, she was boosting him up her list of potential hubby material because he *wasn't* her fantasy man.

Kim knew the difference between fantasy and reality. Fantasies were all about lust—and she knew firsthand that lust didn't make for lifelong commitment. Compatibility did that, and while Gabe didn't make her want to rip off the red thong she'd indulged in during the last semiannual sale at Victoria's Secret, he'd already aced five of *Redbook*'s Perfect Mate Compatibility Requirements. He was an educated, health-conscious, nonsmoking, white-collar professional ready to settle down and start a family.

Gabe ate a piece of cucumber dipped in bean curd and dabbed at his mouth with the corner of his napkin before smoothing it over his lap. Kim's gaze dropped to her own lap, to the neatly spread napkin. *Compulsively neat.* Hello number six.

Six out of the ten. That put him one over her only

other serious prospect, Benny Remington, a brilliant nonsmoking orthodontist desperate to marry and make his mama a grandma before he turned forty.

Kim could sympathize. Her thirty-fifth birthday—a major traumatic event that would make her the oldest single woman working at the high school if she didn't do something *now*—was just around the corner.

One month.

She fought down a wave of rising panic. She would make her deadline to meet and marry before then. She'd already signed up for every major dating service from eHarmony to LassoThatCowboy.com. Sure, she wasn't looking for a working cowboy, per se. But a ranch owner or a horse breeder . . . Someone in charge of the work rather than busting his ass doing the work . . . Now that's what she wanted.

But first she had to decide between Gabe and Benny.

Gabe was definitely leading the race, despite the clear nail polish tipping his fingers. He was probably just a closet nail biter. She'd seen Donna down at the nail salon paint many a man's nails, even in a town like Rebel. It helped with the nail biting, she'd told Kim while painting a flower on her big toe. That, or they were secretly sexually confused and the clear nail polish helped them nurture their feminine side without actually coming out of the closet.

Okay, so Donna hadn't shared that last theory. Miss Esther, the ancient librarian at the high school, had offered up her two cents on that one while getting her sideburns waxed.

Gabe was good. Appropriate. *Decent.*

That's what her mother would have said—God rest her soul.

"There ain't no such thing as fireworks, baby girl," her mother had said too many times to count. *"The best you can hope for is a decent man who'll bring home the bacon and treat you with respect."*

At fifteen, Kim had been hesitant to jump on the decent bandwagon. The thrill of a crush had kicked decent's ass every time. But after nearly twenty years of interacting with the opposite sex and getting her heart crushed by all those crushes, she was starting to think that maybe, just maybe, her mother had been on to something even if the woman hadn't been an expert in the longevity department.

Surely all of those hits and misses when it came to men had taught her something.

Namely that when it came to marriage, chemistry just didn't figure in. After being divorced a record five times, her mother sure as hell knew what didn't work. She had a long list of indecent men behind her, Kim's father included.

No, decent was good. Reliable.

Besides, as well as being decent, Gabe was nice, financially solvent, and he'd asked her out for date number two. *And* he hadn't brought his mother this time.

Hey, a girl had to give credit where credit was due.

He ate several more pieces of watercress in the same ritual fashion—eat, dab, smooth—before eyeing her side of the platter. "You're not going to eat yours, are you? Mother couldn't make it tonight, so I told her I'd bring her a doggie bag."

Okay, so maybe there was such a thing as too decent. Too dependable. Too . . . boring.

The notion followed her through a gluten-free raspberry cupcake that tasted more like a hockey puck than an actual dessert, all the way back to the barn to check in on the animals.

"You're here at nine o'clock on a Thursday night," said the redhead refilling the hay bin in the tack room. "Which means only one thing."

"I'm a dedicated, conscientious teacher?"

"He brought his mother." Tammy Lynn wasn't just a rough and tough redhead who used to ride the barrel racing circuit. She was a perceptive one.

Kim shrugged. "She had previous plans." She handed over a takeout container filled with gluten-free wheat-germ cakes. "I figured the pigs might benefit more from this than me. We're trying to shave off a few pounds so that Oreo can make weight before the Kendall County prospect show next month. I think Tom," he was her sixteen-year-old owner, "has been giving her too many supplements."

"Stop trying to change the subject. Tell," Tammy Lynn said, pulling off her gloves and dusting off her T-shirt.

"Trust me, you don't want to know."

Tammy Lynn wiggled her eyebrows. "Too juicy?"

"Too depressing. His mother couldn't make it tonight, but he assured me she'd be ready, willing, and able for date number three before he rushed home to watch the nightly news with her."

Tammy Lynn sniffed at the to-go bag, then wrinkled her nose. "How can people eat this stuff?"

"It's good for you."

"The only thing good for me is a megadose of sugar and caffeine." She put the bag aside and reached for a thermos full of sweet tea.

Taking a huge swig, she swallowed and sighed. "I still don't understand this whole health food thing."

"I told you. I'm rethinking my health."

"Your mom didn't die because of her diet. She had a heart attack."

"That might have been prevented had she followed a better diet."

"And maybe it was just her time to go. Whether or not pizza with extra cheese was involved didn't matter. I hate to say it about Gabe, but I told you so. He's a total nut job."

"He's not a nut job."

"He's boring," Tammy Lynn pointed out.

"Boring can be good."

"So sayeth the woman who specializes in the subject. You need to get a life, Kim, not another dating service. Get yourself some skinny jeans and a tank top and hit the local honky-tonk. You've got the figure for it."

"My butt is too big."

"Men like a little cush for the push."

"And my boobs are too small."

"Nothing a few gel inserts can't fix."

"And my thighs are too wide."

"That's what the skinny jeans are for. And make sure you get them starched." She indicated the denim hugging her ample thighs. "The stiffer the starch, the more control. They hold it all in. Besides, no man is going to be looking at your thighs if you let that long blond hair of yours down and show 'em a little cleavage. Men don't focus on flaws. They go for the overall picture. You should stop all this health stuff—"

"It's called a life makeover."

"Whatever. You should just stop it, head to Bud's, and suck down some drinks. Life is too short."

"That's my point. It doesn't have to be."

"So sayeth a grade-A control freak."

"I'm not a control freak. I just feel like I need to *do* something."

"Exactly. Control freak. I hope you at least told Gabe where to get off," Tammy Lynn went on. "He's bad enough on his own without bringing his equally boring mother." When Kim just shrugged, Tammy Lynn gave her a pointed stare. "You did tell him to eff off, didn't you?"

"Not exactly."

"Okay, so you said it a bit more tactfully, but you still said it, right?"

"Sort of." When Tammy Lynn frowned, she added, "I know, I know. I shouldn't have agreed to another date, but it's not like I've got anything better to do. We're just going to karaoke at the VFW Hall next week. His mom likes to sing Lady Gaga."

"I take it back. That might not be so boring after all. In fact, maybe I'll swing by. Does she dress up, too?"

"Just stop it." She shook her head. "I'm pathetic, huh? Not for going out with Gabe, though—he's turning out to be just what I'm looking for in a man. Although he is a little too attached to his mother."

"Cord syndrome. She hasn't cut him loose and he doesn't have the balls to do it himself."

Tammy Lynn took another swig of tea. "And you're not pathetic. A little desperate maybe, but still a notch up from pathetic. Pathetic is not having a date—boring loser or otherwise—for seven months, six days, and four hours."

"Roger hasn't called?"

"Not for seven months, six days, and four hours." She sighed, a low, pitiful sound that roused the four goats chewing at a hay bale. They trotted over to the fence and started whining to Tammy Lynn who pulled a piece of apple from her T-shirt pocket and watched it disappear in one gulp.

"It's good to see that you're not obsessing." It was supposed to be a joke, but Tammy Lynn didn't crack a smile.

She simply sighed again, louder this time.

"I'm spending so much time playing Candy Crush, my family is plotting an intervention," the older woman added.

"You really miss him, don't you?"

"Are you kidding? I'd had it with all his snoring and burping and I won't even mention what he did at my mother's house after he ate three bowls of her five-alarm chili." She shook her head. "I've had better sex all by myself." Her voice lowered a notch and her expression grew more thoughtful. "What I really miss the most is having a warm body waiting at home."

Amen to that.

"Someone to talk to," Tammy Lynn went on. "Laugh with, smile at. Someone to just *be there*." Tammy Lynn took another drink. "You'd think with all the hookup sites, that it would be easier to find someone. I've been on FarmersOnly.com and a dozen others, and nothing has worked."

Don't I know it?

Kim ditched the thought and held tight to her optimism. "You'll find someone, just like I have."

"You're making me feel worse."

"I don't mean it like that. You'll find someone perfect for you the way Gabe is perfect for me."

"That's not much better."

"You'll be okay." She changed tactics. "We both will. We just can't get discouraged."

"What about horny? Can we get horny because I'm already there. Even a vibrator doesn't help. Twelve inches sucks without a pair of arms for cuddling after the fact."

"I like 'em twelve inches myself," said the sixtysomething man who rounded the corner, a briefcase in his hand. "There's nothing like a foot-long with extra onions and chili to really rev up the old system. And don't forget the sauerkraut."

Tammy Lynn winked at Kim before turning a smile on Arthur Wallis Sawyer, the school's principal and resident wiener connoisseur.

"Can't say that I've tried any with sauerkraut, but it sounds interesting. So what's up, Principal Sawyer? You pulling a late night, too?"

"Can't have you teachers showing me up." His gaze shifted to Kim and his smile widened. "Both of my best teachers hard at work on a Thursday night? Why, you guys are making me look like a slacker."

Both, as in Cade Thompson, Athletics department supervisor and head football coach. He was rough and tough and just this side of a caveman, or so the rumors suggested. Kim couldn't say herself because she'd exchanged little more than pleasantries with him during the six months he'd been at Rebel High. Cade was more of a yeller than a talker, as any varsity football player would say.

"So where is he?" Kim asked.

"Locked up in the field house, plotting our opening season ass kicking against Travis High School, bless his competitive soul. Speaking of planning, please tell me that you've finished your lesson plan for the fall. I have to submit it to the school district for approval first thing Monday morning."

"Geez, Principal Art, Kim's got a life, you know. Her existence doesn't revolve around this place. She's on a manhunt."

"A manhunt?" His gaze shifted to Kim. "You're hunting for a man? Is this true, Miss Bowman?"

"I thought it high time I settled down."

"Meaning," Tammy Lynn cut in, "her biological clock is ticking and she's starting to get desperate."

"I'm not desperate. I'm simply looking for more than just twelve inches." Kim wanted someone who would like and respect her for who she was. Someone who wouldn't be disappointed once the lust faded, because of who she wasn't. Someone completely opposite every man her mother had ever brought home. "As for that lesson plan," she glanced at her watch, "I can finish it up tonight if I get started now."

He nodded enthusiastically. There were only three things that never failed to nab the principal's attention—work and food and football.

"Get to it, Kim!" He waved his briefcase before saying good night and heading back down the concrete stretch leading out of the barn.

"Do you believe that guy?" Tammy Lynn said once he was out of earshot. "He leaves us here slaving away while he waltzes home."

"Well, you *do* work the night shift."

"That's beside the point."

"Which is?"

"You don't." Tammy Lynn looked at her pointedly.

"Tonight I do." She left Tammy Lynn and headed through the parking lot to the main building. Inside, she flashed her ID badge and headed to her classroom on the second floor.

After flipping on all the lights, she sank down at her desk and keyed her computer. The blank lesson plan flashed in front of her and she damned herself for not working on it sooner. But she'd been busy working on something much more important.

Her future.

Not that the rest of her colleagues would get that.

And that was the problem in a nutshell.

One that had reared its ugly head a few months back when Mr. Sheffield had had his heart attack and she'd been promoted to head of the Ag department.

She'd never really noticed how dark, how quiet, how utterly *empty* her place was until she'd rushed home, bursting at the seams with the good news, and found no one to share it with except her next-door neighbor, the elderly Mr. Camper. And he'd already been sound asleep, so she'd had no one to listen to her, to smile at her, to pat her on the back and tell her she'd finally made it.

Her mother was gone, passed away just last year from a massive heart attack caused by clogged arteries, and Kim herself had always been too busy with her students, too driven, too focused, to have time for a goldfish much less a man.

Until now.

While her professional life was looking up, personally, things couldn't get much worse and she had a freezer full of Single Sensation frozen entrees to prove it.

No more.

She was finding herself a significant other *before* she hit the big three-five.

Her thoughts shifted to Gabe and Benny.

She was well on her way with two hot prospects. All right, so they were more lukewarm than hot, but it wasn't about lust.

Standing in the employee lounge she'd heard her share of war stories regarding catastrophic dates. There was the boring date with the guy who talked nonstop about his hobby—collecting napkins from truck stops all over the country. The blind date with the guy who sucked his teeth. The infuriating date with the guy who argued religion all night. The depressing date with the guy who plotted revenge against his cheating ex. The date that qualified more as a lesson in tactical maneuvers with the guy who had fast hands.

And lips.

And she still hadn't gotten over the news of what he'd tried to do with his big toe.

And all because women had it wrong when they were looking for a husband. They let lust and chemistry dominate the search.

Forget a man who wanted to bang the crap out of her. She wanted a man who *liked* her.

Like how great she looked wearing her ratty old TEXAS A & M sweatshirt. And how great she smelled when she'd been pitching hay in the Ag barn all day. And how she really, really didn't need to worry about her weight because her size 14 hips were just fine as is.

Like. That's what she was looking for. Mutual like between two compatible people.

Her gaze went to the romance novel she'd confiscated from Susie Branders earlier that day. A hunky cowboy blazed on the cover.

Okay, so a good-looking compatible man wouldn't be completely frowned on.

But it wasn't a priority.

It was all about goodness and decency and . . .

Gabe.

He was it and she needed to accept that fact. No matter how unsettling the notion.

CHAPTER 19

It was a terrible night for a stakeout.

The moon was full, the stars bright, both of which made for poor cover for anyone trying to stay out of sight.

Silvery beams pushed down through the trees and illuminated the old truck and the smokestack that protruded from the rusted-out bed. Smoke whispered from the opening, fading into the sky like warm breath on a cold night.

Yep, it was a terrible night for a stakeout and prime time to get his ass blown to smithereens.

Hunter let the binoculars fall around his neck and shrank back behind the trees a good fifty yards away from ground zero. He couldn't risk moving in closer, not with the game camera blinking on a nearby tree and the visibility of the full moon.

Seeing what was actually going on was going to be more difficult, so he was going to have to rely on his other senses.

Water trickled from a nearby stream, blending with the crickets that buzzed. His ears perked and he tuned his hearing, peeling away the various sounds until he heard the crackle of a fire. He couldn't see anything with the old shell of the truck hiding what was underneath, but he knew there was a fire burning, feeding smoke through the pipe. They were brewing, which meant it wasn't the Mayweather brothers because they were tucked away at home with a deep-dish pizza and a triple-threat brownie from the local Papa John's. They'd been fired, all right.

Which meant someone had to have taken their place.

He eased slowly to the left, picking his way silently until he had a better vantage point.

He held up the binoculars, sweeping the area again until he finally noted the small round globe that perched on a tree branch nearby. It blended in for the most part, but Hunter had seen enough cameras to know one when he saw it. He studied the area, looking for more but there was just the one. It reflected a ray of moonlight that pushed down through the trees at just the right angle and stood out when it might have otherwise blended in.

Biding his time, he moved a safe distance around the perimeter, straining to hear voices or any indication that there were actual people nearby.

There had to be. The still was brewing so someone had to be tending it.

A faint thud, like metal hitting metal, pushed past the crickets and he stiffened. He watched as one of the old truck doors opened and a man emerged. He wore a base-ball cap pulled low and a plaid shirt, the sleeves rolled up above his elbows. He dumped a jug full of liquid onto the ground before disappearing back inside the cab of the truck. His head bobbed and disappeared and Hunter knew the truck was just a cover for the still set up be-low, probably in a cave dug into the earth, the truck parked on top like a forgotten relic from the past year's flood.

No one would suspect what was going on underneath.

Hunter fell back, backtracking for the next one hundred yards until he knew he was a safe distance away, and then he waited for the next few hours until he heard voices and the distant grumble of a four-wheeler. The engine idled a few moments before fading slowly but surely until . . . nothing.

He moved cautiously then, easing his way until he reached his previous spot. A quick look-see through the binoculars and he noted that the smoke had disappeared. The dome still gleamed in the moonlight, but the game camera nearby had been opened up, the outer shell hanging open to reveal that the inside had been removed.

No doubt they were going to check the footage to make sure there'd been no Peeping Toms.

His attention shifted to the small lock that was still hooked in the opening. It hung open, waiting for the camera's return. Another glance at the dome camera and he moved to the left, tracking back behind the field of vision so that he could come up on the game cam setup from behind.

He reached around the tree and touched the small padlock. A quick lift and he retrieved the piece of hardware. It was round with a digital display rather than the traditional key lock. Too expensive for the average hunter, which meant it might be a viable lead.

Sliding the metal into his pocket, he backtracked around the area, careful to stay away from the truck and the dome camera's field of vision.

It took time, but soon he was in the clear. He made

his way back through the trees for the next two miles, deep into the dense foliage that eventually led to the road and his SUV parked on the shoulder.

Climbing inside, he checked his cell phone, noted the text from Marge reminding him that he had a granola bar in the glove compartment and one from Bobby telling him that Kaitlyn was excited at the prospect of a date with him. All she needed was a day and time.

Tomorrow night.

That's what Bobby suggested. He was planning a double date and Friday was steak night at the Beef-it-up Diner, a new steakhouse out on the interstate.

Yes.

That's what he wanted to text back. His muscles were tight. His body tense. His gut inside out. And all because of a certain blonde and some really hot kisses.

That meant he needed to kiss someone else. To get Jenna Tucker out of his system and set his sights on someone else. On someone appropriate.

Not because he cared what anyone else thought of him.

This wasn't about his reputation. It was about preserving his own sanity. About forgetting the past and staying focused on the future.

Jenna reminded him too much of the man he'd once been.

All the more reason to let Bobby fix him up with Kaitlyn.

He would, but not tomorrow night. Maybe next week. When things had died down and hopefully, he'd busted the moonshiners he was after.

The last thing he needed was a distraction.

He needed to head back to the station, flag the evidence, and see what he could find out about it.

He would.

But he had one stop to make first.

He'd meant to drop off the door the other night, but then he'd been sidetracked with another wild kiss. Tonight he was installing the door and then he was out of there.

No touching.

No kissing.

Nothing.

That's what he told himself.

He just hoped like hell he managed to remember it when he found himself face to face with sexy Jenna Tucker.

My dearest P.J.,

I know writing these letters is futile. You'll never receive them since I haven't been able to talk Martha into sneaking them out to the post office. She's too afraid of our folks and I can't say that I blame her. Father has become unbearable, especially now that I'm starting to show. It's only a matter of time before he refuses to look at me at all and I'm sent away to my aunt Luella's in Chicago. She already has a room ready. I'm to stay with her until the baby comes and the church steps in. They are going to take the baby, or so my father says. But I will not let such a thing happen. This is my baby. All I have left of the man I love. I can't lose this baby and its father. I won't. I will find a way out. A way back. I will give this baby a mother and a father if it's the last thing I do.

Still begging your forgiveness,

Clara Bell Sawyer

Jenna folded the letter and tried to ignore the strange hollowness in her stomach. The sadness. Poor Clara Bell.

Jenna couldn't imagine being so young and isolated and at the mercy of so many people who thought they knew what was best. Sure, she was surrounded by an entire town that thought they knew what was best for everyone, but she hadn't bent to their will.

Until now.

She stiffened against the thought, stuffed the letter on the bottom of the pile, and set the stack to the side. She spent the next hour working her way through the cupboards on the left side of the kitchen, boxing up plates and dishes and a stash of small appliances that she'd forgotten existed.

An ancient waffle maker her mother had used when she'd made Sunday breakfast. An old juicer that had belonged to her grandmother. Back during a time when James Harlin might have actually drank something healthy rather than pickling his liver with his homemade shine. An old hand-cranked mixer Callie had used to make lumpy mashed potatoes when she'd first started cooking for the family.

They'd been the most godawful things, but she and Brandy had eaten them anyway because they'd had nothing and no one else. James Harlin certainly hadn't lifted a hand to cook for his orphaned granddaughters.

Her stomach grumbled as she closed the box and set it to the side. She pushed to her feet. Her hand went to the freezer, but she let it fall away. She needed something stronger than Callie's sorbet.

She thought of the ice cream sandwiches stuffed at

the back of the freezer. Cool and sweet and oh so satisfying.

But not satisfying enough.

Her gaze went to the cupcakes. She'd promised herself no more until tomorrow. At the rate she was going, she wouldn't have to worry about Hunter wanting her. A daily dose of cupcakes and she'd be a good fifty pounds heavier in no time. Instant turn-off.

That's what she told herself, but she couldn't shake the gut feeling that it would take more than a few extra pounds to dissuade a man like Hunter. Not when he set his sights on something. On someone.

She grabbed the box and opened the lid.

One cupcake, she promised herself.

Just one.

A few moments later, Jenna sank down on the old porch swing. Wood groaned and chains creaked. A steady squeak scraped across her nerves as she pushed the old two-seater into motion.

Opening the cupcake box, she pulled out the decadent chocolate, peeled back the paper, and took a bite.

Chocolate exploded and a groan worked its way up her throat. Mmm . . .

The first bite was good, but she needed great. Amazing. Phenomenal. Satisfying.

Yep, she needed some satisfaction. Maybe then she could stop thinking about Hunter and how good he'd kissed and how she wanted to kiss him again. And again.

She took another bite. The chocolate stroked her taste buds and she groaned again. Okay, bite two was a little bit better. Her hopes high, she went for number three.

She was down to one last mouthful when she heard the deep familiar voice and her heart stalled.

"Sounds like somebody's enjoying herself."

Not nearly enough.

Not yet.

Her gaze snapped up and collided with a pair of twinkling blue eyes. Her stomach hollowed out and her mouth watered. A craving whispered through her, skimming her nerve endings and setting her entire body on fire. A feeling that had nothing to do with the cupcake and everything to do with the hot, sexy man who stood in front of her.

CHAPTER 20

"That must be one amazing cupcake," Hunter said, his legs making quick work of the yard that separated them.

A few seconds later, the swing dipped as he sank down next to Jenna and her stalled heart revved and bolted forward at breakneck speed.

"I could hear you clear across the yard," Hunter added.

His jeans-clad thigh brushed hers and . . . uh-oh. He was wearing jeans. No boring-schmoring beige uniform tonight. Worn black jeans and a soft black T-shirt that stretched across his broad shoulders and hugged his muscular biceps. He also wore a grin that said while he might be referring to the frosted goodie in her hand, he was thinking about something a lot more decadent when he said, "You were really into it."

"It's okay," she managed after a distinct swallow. "I . . . That is," another swallow and she managed, "what are you doing here?"

"Your door, remember?"

"You don't have to . . ." she started, but then he caught her hand and the words scrambled.

"I promised. I know it's just going to get torn down, but it's nothing expensive. Just a good temporary to replace your old door until the demolition. So how about it?"

"About what?"

"Are you going to give me a taste of whatever it is that's got you oohing and ahhing?"

She held out the last bite. "Help yourself."

He took the cake, popped it into his mouth, and swallowed in one big gulp.

"See? It's good, right? Chocolate Nirvana. One of Brandy's specialties."

"Your sister really knows her way around an oven!"

"She's been baking since she was a kid. She used to fire up the stove every afternoon to make brownies or cookies or something. Our house always smelled like sugar."

"My mom wasn't much for baking," Hunter said, his thigh brushing hers as the swing moved back and forth in a motion that was almost hypnotic. Her muscles eased and for the first time in weeks, she found herself relaxing. "She didn't cook much either. She was always working."

"Your mom was a paralegal, right?"

He nodded. "That's how she met and married my dad. They worked together and so most nights were TV dinners for me and my brother when we were kids."

"What about when you got older?"

"I ran on pure adrenaline most of the time. Food didn't figure in. And when it did, it was usually burgers or chicken. You know, something fast."

"I would have given anything for a burger instead of

Callie's mashed potatoes. She wasn't much of a cook at first. She got better as the years went on. That, or we just got used to eating her stuff. Poor Brett."

A warm chuckle sizzled over her nerve endings. "He doesn't look the worse for wear. In fact, he looks damned good. I saw him the other day. He's never looked so happy."

"It's crazy, right? They're both from opposite sides of the fence, but they're happy. I think Callie might be pregnant." The words were out before she could stop them and she immediately caught her lip, trying to figure out why she'd blurted out something so important.

Private.

Because there was something mesmerizing about the steady motion of the swing and the close proximity of his warm body.

"I shouldn't have said that. She just doesn't know for sure and I'm sure she wouldn't want people talking—"

"Your secret's safe with me, Jenna."

Silence closed in around them for a long moment and then the words started coming again, pouring out of her mouth of their own accord. "They're going to tear down the house in a matter of days. I've got most everything out, but I'm still not ready."

"A lot more packing to go?"

"Packing's the easy part." It was the letting go she was having more trouble with. The saying goodbye. The change. "As long as you've got plenty of boxes," she rushed on, desperate to ignore the sudden rush of thoughts. "I need to pick up more. A lot more. Speaking of which, I should really get back inside—"

"But we're not done here."

"What's that supposed to mean?"

"The cupcake was good, but I really need something else, he said, pushing to his feet.

"Like what?"

The swing bounced and shook as he turned and dropped to his knees in front of her. He reached for the waistband of her shorts. "Like this."

"I don't think . . ." she started, but then one strong finger touched her lips and she tasted salty skin and hot, sexy male.

"You think too much." He unfastened the button and shimmied the material down her legs, his fingers grazing her sensitive skin along the way. "You're too wound up. You need to try to relax. Forget the packing for a little while and just feel."

"I . . ." She wanted to. She really did. But she'd spent her teenage years doing just that and it had gotten her nothing except a big, bad reputation.

And a few good memories, a voice whispered. She'd definitely had fun.

And suddenly a little harmless fun didn't seem like such a bad thing. It wasn't as if she was riding through town in front of God and the entire senior women's prayer group. She was in back of her own house, away from the gossips and goodie-goodies.

Hunter was the only one here. In front of her. Surrounding her. Begging her to open up.

And she couldn't help herself.

She did just that.

Her thighs fell open and he wedged himself between her knees. Heat swept through her and chased the oxygen from her lungs as his fingertips swept from her calves, up the outside of her knees, until his hands came to rest on her thighs.

"I've been wanting to do this for a very long time."

"We only really met a few days ago."

"Yeah, well it seems like fucking forever being so close to you and not touching you." He touched his lips to the inside of her thigh just a few inches shy of her panties. "Not tasting you."

He nibbled and licked and worked his way slowly toward the heart of her. She found herself opening her legs even wider, begging him closer.

He trailed his tongue over the silk veering her wet heat and pushed the material into her slit until her lips plumped on either side. "Christ, you're so beautiful." He trailed a fingertip over the sensitive flesh and a shiver gripped her. Her breath caught and she braced one hand on his shoulder. Her fingers curled into the sinewy flesh.

Her body tightened. Nerves pulsed, vibrated, faster and faster. Until she was wound so tight that she just knew she would shatter at any moment.

She didn't.

Because it wasn't enough.

There were too many barriers between them. Too many clothes.

As if he read her thoughts, he gripped the edge of her panties and she lifted her hips to accommodate him. The satin material slithered down her legs and landed in a puddle near her feet.

He caught her ankles and urged her knees over his

shoulders. Large, strong hands slid under her ass and drew her to the edge of the swing. He tilted her just enough to better the angle and then he dipped his head.

He parted her with his tongue and lapped at her sensitive clit. He tasted and savored, his tongue stroking, plunging, driving her mindless until she came apart beneath him. A cry vibrated from her throat and joined the symphony of crickets that surrounded them.

Her heart beat a frantic pace for the next few moments as she tried to come to terms with what had just happened.

She'd said to hell with her transformation and backslid right back into her old ways.

That's what she told herself, but she felt too alive, too friggin' *good* to care at the moment.

Because as wrong as Hunter DeMassi was for her, he felt very right.

So much so that she closed her eyes and leaned her head back. She forgot all about the house and the packing and the letting go and just let the orgasm ripple over her for a long, delicious moment.

"We should take this inside," he said when she managed to open her eyes.

Yes. That's what she meant to say.

They should be inside, hidden away from anyone who might happen by because she had a newly won reputation to protect and so did he and, well, it wasn't like they were a couple.

"I—I really don't think we should be doing this." The words came of their own accord, fueled by a crazy sense of hurt because they were all wrong for each other and he obviously knew it as much as she did.

And that's bad because . . . ?

It wasn't. At least he wasn't mentally planning a wedding like all the other nice guys in her past.

But then Hunter wasn't so nice. She could see that now despite the front he put up. He was every bit the bad boy that fueled her fantasies.

Worse because all those bad-ass ways were wrapped up in a nice, respectable package. A man she could fall for. Lose her heart to.

She shot down the notion as soon as it reared its ugly head. One decent orgasm and she was already picking out china. Talk about hard up.

"I—I really should get back to work. I'm cleaning out kitchen cabinets." She tugged on her shorts while he pushed to his feet. She scrambled to an upright position and fought with the button at her waistband.

"You're kidding, right?"

"Not that I didn't enjoy it." She snatched up her undies from the ground. "I did, but I shouldn't have because you and I . . . Well, it just can't happen. I'm really trying to change my image and, well, I don't do one-night stands anymore."

"Maybe I want more than a one-night stand."

She pinned him with a stare. "I don't do relationships either. Not right now. Things are too up in the air. I'm trying to get my life in order and this will only complicate things."

"You're right." He reached for her waistband and slid the button easily into place, his gaze dark and knowing as he stared down at her.

As if he saw all the fears inside.

As if he shared them.

"You're not my type and I'm not yours and this really is a bad idea. I should get busy with that door. That's why I stopped by."

Before she could respond, he kissed her roughly on the lips and headed for the house.

Jenna thought about following him, but that would just lead to another kiss and maybe another orgasm and, well, talk about a *really* bad idea.

She sank down onto the swing and settled in for the next hour, until she heard the rumble of his SUV in the distance and the fade of the engine as he headed back to town.

Yep, Hunter DeMassi was a bad idea. The worst she'd had in a long, long time.

And damned if that didn't make her want him that much more.

She thought about the letters, about how Clara fooled her family into thinking that she was the perfect daughter. But deep down, she never changed. She never stopped loving the father of her child. She never stopped begging P.J. for his forgiveness.

Because deep down, she'd been the same wild, wanton girl who'd fallen in love with him in the first place.

Now and always . . .

The truth followed Jenna back inside, along with her unsatisfied hunger, and ate at her as she tried to pack up the kitchen and convince herself that she was really and truly making progress.

Cleaning up her life.

Changing it.

But deep down, she couldn't shake the gut feeling that she was the same girl she'd always been. That she was stuck. In the same town with the same reputation and the same uncontrollable urges that had led her down the wild and wicked path in the first place.

If only that notion still bothered her half as much as it once had.

CHAPTER 21

Hunter stared at the ceiling and fought the urge to pull on some clothes and haul ass back to Jenna's place. The taste of her lingered on his lips, and no amount of evidence, no matter how promising, could distract him.

He'd found a viable lead. The local Ace Hardware store carried the exact lock from the game cam, but they sold very few. So few in fact that it wouldn't be hard for Bucky Ambrose, the store's owner, to track all the purchases over the past year.

Not tonight, of course. Bucky and his woman were playing poker with two other couples and he certainly wasn't going to bail just to help out Hunter. But tomorrow . . . He would get on it first thing Friday morning and turn over a list of names of all the people who'd purchased the lock since he'd started carrying it.

In the meantime, Hunter could do nothing but wait. And think. And want.

Fuck.

He threw off the sheet and climbed out of bed. It was just past midnight and the night was dark. Quiet. If he'd been farther away from the main hub of town. But he'd taken a place just down the street from the station, directly across from the Dairy Queen. The place was just closing their drive-thru and so the lights were still on, a few cars still left in the parking lot.

He pulled the drapes on the front bedroom window closed and turned to pull on a T-shirt and jeans. A few minutes later, he grabbed his keys and headed for the pickup truck that sat in the driveway next to his regulation SUV. The truck was old. Worn. Hell, he should have gotten rid of it ages ago, but it still ran pretty good and, well, he hadn't gotten around to placing an ad so the Chevy still sat in the same spot.

A few clicks and the engine turned over. He gave it some gas and listened to the motor grumble and sputter back to life. Shifting into Reverse, he backed out of the drive and pulled out onto the street. Ten minutes later, he was speeding down the nearest farm road, headed past the city limits. He wasn't sure where he was going. He just knew he needed to drive.

Until he stopped thinking about Jenna.

Wanting her.

Needless to say, an hour later he was still behind the wheel, still running from his demons, still wanting *her*.

He fixed his gaze on the road, but in his mind's eye, he saw Jenna.

Her face flushed, her eyes heavy-lidded, her lips parted on a moan. She was open and trembling in front of him, the scent of her sweet sex so potent and ripe in his nostrils, her soft pink folds glistening in the moonlight.

Hunger knifed through him and he shifted on the seat to give his hard-on more room. Right. He was damn near bursting and there was no relief in sight.

Working at the button of his jeans, he slid the waist-band open and shoved his zipper down. His erection bobbed forward, pushing against the soft cotton of his boxer briefs. Fingertips grazed the hard bulge and a gasp caught on his lips.

He wanted her, all right, more than he'd ever wanted any woman.

And she wanted him. That's what his gut told him, but damned if she wasn't resisting.

She was trying to clean up her image, to change, just as he'd tried so long ago, and she didn't want to want a man like him. He couldn't blame her. That creek ran both ways. She was the worst type of woman in the world, one who called to his baser instincts, who reminded him of how good it felt to be so bad.

Sex, he reminded himself. This was all about sex and the all-important fact that he hadn't really done the deed in a long time. It made sense that he would be losing his freakin' mind at this point.

All he needed was to cut loose for a few hours. Just drive somewhere, pick up someone, and stick his cock so deep he stopped thinking about anyone and anything except busting a nut. Just once.

There was a bar on the outskirts of Austin that he'd frequented back in the day. He could drive over and bam, problem solved.

But instead of driving straight and hitting the main interstate, he found himself out by the rodeo arena.

The place was still lit with a handful of stragglers trying to get in a few more precious hours of practice. Hunter pulled into a parking spot and crossed the gravel lot until he reached the main corral.

He spent the next hour watching the cowboys work the bucking broncs. They weren't very good, but he had to give them an A for effort. Particularly when it came to Hell Raiser. The horse was brutal, bucking and kicking and nearly giving one of the men a concussion.

But then that was the point.

For the horse to throw such a fit that only the roughest, toughest cowboy could survive atop him.

Hunter had been that cowboy once upon a time. He'd been riding his way up the ladder, winning a few purses here and there, hoping for a break that would take him straight to the professional circuit.

But his brother had died before he'd hit a major rodeo and so he'd given up his dream and straightened up his act by settling down and getting a real job.

He eyed the animal, the lather covering the mane, the gleaming hind legs, the power packed into such a ferocious package.

He could practically feel the heat beneath him, the strength, the desire.

He ducked his head into a nearby watering trough and held himself under until his lungs burned as badly as the rest of his body. He came up sputtering, gasping for air. The coolness dribbled down his neck and shoulders and drip-dropped onto his heated skin.

But it did nothing to cool his body temperature. He was too wired. Too damned hot.

Before he knew what was happening, he found himself perched on the corral fence, the horse standing idly nearby. So calm and deceiving.

As if she wouldn't throw a fit the second she felt his weight on her back.

"Sheriff?" The voice caught him just before he slid down into the corral and crossed the distance to the animal. "Is that you?"

He turned to see Buzz Trayhill Sawyer standing nearby. He was the trainer in charge of the bucking horses. A nice guy in his midforties. He'd been just starting out as a hand back when Hunter had been riding, and now he took care of every bronc to come through the arena.

"Hey, there." Hunter gave him a wave. "How's it going?"

"Not too bad. What are you doing out here?" He frowned. "Is everything all right? Jack and Larry aren't fighting again?" Jack and Larry were two local riders who routinely went at it to the point that the authorities were called and Hunter had to come out and settle yet another Tucker/Sawyer dispute.

"No, no. This isn't an official call. I was driving by and just thought I'd stop in and see if everything was okay."

"We're doing fine. Got a rodeo tomorrow night so the cowboys are putting in a few late hours to make sure they qualify." He waved a hand at the nearby men. "I don't need to tell you. I'm sure you remember how that is."

He did now. He'd locked all those feelings away and ignored them for the most part until Jenna Tucker had stirred him up and made him feel so restless inside.

Anxious.

Desperate.

Buzz smiled. "Want to take a ride?" He pointed to Hell Raiser. "For old time's sake?"

His hands itched and it was all he could do not to hit the dust and make his way to the horse. "I'll pass," he managed, climbing down off the railing until he stood on the outside of the fence. "I need to head back. See you later."

"See ya, Sheriff."

Hunter passed by the watering trough and ignored the urge to duck his head under again and douse the thoughts burning him up from the inside out.

The restlessness.

No amount of water was going to cool the fire that burned inside of him. There was only one cure for that and as much as he wanted to deny it, he knew he was going to have to do something about it.

He needed to have sex.

And he needed it fast.

CHAPTER 22

For the first time in a long time, Hunter DeMassi was out on a Friday night.

Not sitting in a squad car or parked at the weekly VFW spaghetti dinner or watching the local high school football game, but *out* out.

He sat smack-dab in the middle of the local honky-tonk, a bottle of beer in front of him, a lively Jason Aldean song bouncing off the walls around him, and all because the past few days had been eating him up from the inside out.

Seeing Jenna every night for the past week when he'd stopped by to check in on her and not kissing her again, tasting her, was eating away at his determination.

To the point that he'd said to hell with everything and hauled ass here when he should be trudging through the woods, keeping an eye on the still site.

The questions rolled around in his brain, but he wasn't in the mood to sort through them. There were too many *maybes* and *could bes* and damn, but there were a lot of people here.

He glanced around and ignored the strange tightening in his gut. The sliver of excitement because he hadn't been inside these walls since last year when he'd picked up old Marvin Shumaker Sawyer, the town drunk and a distant cousin, for forgetting to pull up his pants after a trip to the restroom. He'd exposed himself and the bartender had called it in.

The place had changed little since the call. It sat just up the road from the local rodeo arena and so the place was stuffed with local cowboys. And lots of cowboys meant lots of women.

Locals, he reminded himself.

Which wasn't a good idea at all.

But then neither was this.

All he had to do was scope out the sea of hot bodies that filled the dance floor and pick whichever one caught his fancy. A blond bombshell with big breasts or a brunette with a nice ass or a redhead with long legs. Someone to take the edge off and ease the damn near constant hard-on making his life freakin' miserable. A good lay and he would stop fantasizing about Jenna.

Then he could think again.

And after the fact? When he had to face the morning after and whichever woman he'd ended up with?

He shook away the nagging question. He was past the point of worrying about that right now. He needed to act first and think later. Just once.

That's what he told himself, but he couldn't quite get his ass off the bar stool long enough to turn his bright idea into reality. He was the sheriff, after all, and he had a reputation to uphold, and so instead of eyeballing a woman he settled for a beer.

He took a deep swig of Coors, but the liquid didn't

ease the tightening in his gut or sate the thirst that clawed at his throat.

So go talk to Sherri Grimes.

She was nice enough. A single schoolteacher who helped out at the local homeless shelter every other weekend. Exactly the type of woman his Mimi would like to see him with.

If he had to fall off the wagon, she was the perfect woman to do it with.

Except he didn't feel the same tightening in his gut when he looked at her. No jolt to his heart. No instant hard-on.

He downed another swig of beer and wished with all his heart that he could punch something.

His gaze fixed on the woman currently two-stepping her way across the dance floor with another man. Wouldn't you know he'd have shitty luck? He'd come to the honky-tonk to escape Jenna.

Yet, here she was, obviously nursing the same bright idea that had hauled him inside the honky-tonk in the first place.

She wore a red tank top that revealed her smooth, silky arms and a pair of fitted jeans that hung low on her hips. Add a pair of blinged-out cowboy boots and Jenna Tucker was definitely the hottest thing in Rebel.

But her appeal went deeper than the sexy getup. Her long blond hair was slightly mussed and flowed down around her shoulders. Her eyes sparkled. Her skin glowed. She looked as if she'd just rolled out of bed after a night of incredible sex.

Which wasn't too far off the mark if there was any truth to her reputation.

For all he knew she'd already done the deed and was blowing off a little steam afterward.

At the same time, she'd done her best to resist him this past week so he wasn't so sure he bought the whole bad-girl picture she'd painted for herself over the years.

He downed another gulp and barely resisted the urge to haul ass across the room and inform her that she had tons of things to do at home so she should stop making a fool of herself and get the hell out of here.

Christ, she was practically melting all over that cowboy.

Her arms looped around his neck. A smile tilted her full lips as she seemed to hang on his every word. Her boots kicked up sawdust and her ass shook as she moved this way and slid that way, dancing as if she hadn't a care in the world.

As if she didn't give a shit about her reputation.

All that recent effort to revamp her image blown to hell and back with one sultry smile and a wag of her hips.

Not that he cared that she was blowing it Hell no. She was a grown woman who could do what she damned well pleased. So what if she was living up to her bad-girl reputation again by fawning all over that guy. She could fawn over any man she chose.

She was a grown woman.

At the same time, it was his civic duty as a public

servant to lend a hand to the constituents in his town. To help them out when they were obviously about to make a big, big mistake.

He was the sheriff, after all. It was his civic obligation to save her from herself when she was obviously about to make a huge mistake. One she would surely regret in the morning because, let's face it, that guy she was with was a bona fide moron.

Before he could bolt to his feet, he felt a tap on his shoulder.

"Sorry, but I'm on duty," he started, turning to see the woman who'd come up behind him. She was sex on a stick, with pretty pouty lips and long, dark hair and a curvy figure.

Perfect for a night of hot, wild, mindless sex.

And all wrong for the sheriff.

"Fancy seeing you here, Sheriff. How about you buy me a drink?"

"I'd love to, but I'm here in a professional capacity."

"What?"

Yeah, what?

He motioned across the dance floor. "I'm on a stakeout," he blurted, lowering his voice and motioning her in closer. "I can't say anymore, but you might want to get out of here before there's any trouble."

Her eyes glittered at the thought. "Really? Something's going down? Right here?"

Actually, something was going up thanks to Jenna and her sexy getup, but Hunter wasn't going to argue semantics. He nodded and motioned toward the door.

"I'd start walking the other way if I were you. I wouldn't want you caught in the cross-fire."

Her excitement turned to worry and she turned, working her way through the maze of tables until she reached a group of women. A few words and they all stood and headed for the Exit.

If only he could get Jenna out of here as fast.

He signaled the bartender to bring him a second round before shifting his gaze back to Jenna.

The minute his attention fixed on her, she stiffened and missed a step. She wobbled and the man's arms tightened around her. His hands snuck around her waist and he pulled her close and . . .

Ah, *hell* no.

He pushed to his feet, and just like that, Hunter gave in to a fierce swell of possessiveness. Regardless of what had—or, in this case, *hadn't* happened in the past between them, right now, at this moment, Jenna was his responsibility.

His, period.

And it was high time she admitted it.

Uh-oh.

Panic bolted through Jenna because it wasn't supposed to happen this way. Hunter wasn't supposed to waltz right up to her as if he had every right. No, he was supposed to see for himself that she was not, in any way shape or form, into him.

At least that had been the plan when she'd first spotted him. She'd initially gone to the honky-tonk because the bakery had been closed, the cupcakes locked up tight, and she hadn't been ready to go home. To face the all but empty house now and the memories that still filled it.

She'd needed to escape and so, against her better judgment and her newfound reputation as a responsible workaholic, she'd pulled on her favorite outfit and hit the local honky-tonk to drown her mixed feelings in a frozen margarita.

That and to forget Hunter and how wildly attracted she was to him.

But then she'd walked in and there he'd sat and bam, suddenly she'd needed to convince him—and herself—that she wasn't desperately attracted to him.

But instead of taking the hint, he was walking straight for her.

She tightened her hold on Jimmy or Joe or John or something with a J and stared into his watered-down blue eyes. He really was a nice guy. Worked on a nearby farm. Went to church every Sunday. The perfect man to prove her point with and have a little innocent fun.

And that's all it was. Innocent.

No way should she feel so *guilty* all of a sudden.

Even if Hunter was headed straight for her, looking as if she'd just eaten the last cookie from his box.

She saw him out of the corner of her eye, a determined shadow that bisected the dance floor and closed the distance between them. Even more, she could feel him.

Her skin prickled and heat skittered up and down her spine. Awareness rippled through her like a wave gunning for shore and it was all she could do not to turn when he stepped up behind her.

"I need to talk to you." His deep voice slid into her ears, pushing aside the music and laughter and the frantic beat of her heart.

She stiffened against the urge to turn, wrap her arms around his neck, and taste him again.

Because one taste would lead to two and two to three and three to a one-night stand that would surely destroy any and all efforts to change the town's perception of her.

That's what scared her the most. It certainly wasn't the possibility that she might *like* sleeping with him. Or that she might want to go back for seconds.

Seconds never figured in with the nice guys she'd been dating lately and while Hunter seemed to be breaking the mold, she wasn't giving up hope yet. He was just like all the other Chuck and Kevins. Nice. *Forgettable.*

She twined her fingers around Jimmy/Joe/John's neck and gave him her most convincing smile. "Don't mind him. He can wait until we finish our dance. As you can see, I'm kind of in the middle of something right now," she told Hunter.

But Hunter wasn't a man to take no for an answer. "It's official police business. If you don't cooperate I'll be obliged to make you."

"You and what army?"

"Just me." He sounded none too pleased and a traitorous slither of joy went through her. For a split second, she entertained the crazy hope that she might actually feel some fireworks. That he might feel them. That he might be jealous. "Either you cooperate or I'll have to arrest you for obstructing justice."

"That's ridiculous."

"That's the law."

"But this is my favorite song?" She gave Jimmy/Joe/John another sorry-about-this look. "I love Luke Bryan."

"This is Jason Aldean."

"Whatever."

"Maybe you should go with him," Jimmy/Joe/John cut in. "It could be important."

"Great advice." Hunter's deep voice sounded a split second before he took her hand. "Now get lost, fella."

"You can't just come in here and ruin my fun." Her voice followed him, but he didn't slow his pace as he strode toward the nearest exit and hauled her behind him.

"I should think you'd want me ruining it. I thought you were trying to change your image?"

"Yeah, well, maybe it's fine just the way it is." She shrugged. "Maybe I'm going out of my mind packing boxes and I needed to get away for a little while."

"Go for ice cream," he growled. "Or get a hamburger. But steer clear of here."

"You're not my boss."

"I'm everyone's boss, sugar. I'm the sheriff." He hit the bar on the exit door, pushed through, and hauled her around the building.

A few more steps and they disappeared around the back, leaving the noise and the music behind. A few more steps and he stopped. She ran into him from behind, her soft curves pressing against him for a quick moment that scrambled his common sense.

"What the hell?" she growled, but the words stopped as he whirled on her. Their eyes clashed. And he knew in that next instant that maybe hauling her outside, away from prying eyes, wasn't the smartest thing to do considering he was horny as hell and she was the hottest thing in the entire state of Texas.

Where Jenna had avoided taking a good look at Hunter inside, she couldn't help but drink in every inch of him now.

He looked so different without his uniform.

So dark and dangerous and . . . uh-oh.

He wore a black T-shirt, faded jeans, and a look that said he was royally pissed and not the least bit inclined to hide it. Tension rolled off his body in huge waves. His jaw clenched. A muscle ticked wildly near his left cheek. His eyes had clouded to a dark, stormy blue, like the sky just before it opened up with a vicious summer thunderstorm and she felt every bit of the electricity that stirred the air.

She ignored the tiny thrill that slid through her and damned her traitorous body. "What's so all-fire important that you had to practically abduct me?"

He inched closer, making her crane her neck to look at him as he towered over her. "You're wrong. Dead wrong."

"About what?"

"About not wanting a one-night stand." His voice lowered a notch. "We're both consenting adults. You're hot and bothered and I'm hot and bothered. There's no reason why we ought to be out looking for other people when it's obvious that we both want the same thing."

Physically.

He punched her buttons and she punched his, and that was the problem in and of itself.

She'd given up the right type because they'd been all wrong. No more bad boys.

At the same time, he just looked like a bad boy. Hunter was every bit the fine, upstanding guy she'd been looking for.

The right man to be seen with.

To fall into bed with.

To fall in love with.

She ditched the last thought. She'd given up on the good guys, too. She had too many things going on in her life to fall in love.

If that were even possible and she wasn't convinced.

She'd never felt it.

She'd never even seen it.

Sure, she knew her parents had loved each other, but she'd been young when they'd died and she didn't really remember anything except her dad out working and her mom up to her elbows with the cooking and cleaning at home. And her grandfather yelling and cussing at them both because he'd been ornery and just plain mean.

Most of the time.

She ignored the strange tightening in her chest and focused on the man standing in front of her. *The right man,* her brain screamed.

But it was the wrong time because Jenna was trying to clean up her image and that meant steering clear of all men.

Her head knew that, but her body wasn't paying attention at the moment.

Her nipples pebbled and her thighs ached.

"You know we should do this." His deep voice slid into her ears, so deep and mesmerizing. His eyes blazed with a hunger that kicked her in the chest and sent the air whooshing from her lungs. "Right here, right now."

Excitement bolted through her, followed by a rush of doubt because while she might *want* to do this, she couldn't.

She swallowed past the sudden lump in her throat. "I really don't think—"

"That's your problem, Jenna. You think too much when it's not about that. It's about this." And then his mouth swooped down and captured hers.

CHAPTER 23

Jenna's heart beat double-time, the sound thundering in her ears, drowning out her conscience and her fear. She slid her arms around his neck and gave in to the passion pounding through her. No more thinking. Just *this*. This man. And what he was doing to her.

With the purposeful slant of his lips. The tantalizing dance of his tongue. The strong splay of his hands at the base of her spine. The muscular wall of his chest crushing her breasts. The hardness of his thighs pressed flush against hers.

Yep, he was doing it all right. Silencing her objections. Stirring her passion. Turning her on so high and so fast that she started to think that maybe he was right. Maybe they should do this. Just this once. If she could satisfy the lust, then maybe she could think straight again.

His lips plundered hers, his tongue pushing deep to stroke and explore and leave her breathless. He pressed her up against the side of the building, her back flat against the cold tin. She felt the pulse of the music from inside, the vibration stirring her excitement.

And then he leaned into her, his body flush against hers, so that she could feel *his* excitement.

He caught the straps of her tank top, shoving them down her arms along with her bra straps, until the material sagged at her waist and her breasts spilled free.

Dipping his head, he caught one rosy nipple between his teeth. He flicked the tip with his tongue before opening his mouth wider. He drew her in and sucked until a moan worked its way up her throat.

He pinned her to the wall, pressing one hard thigh between her legs that forced her wider until she rode him. The denim seemed practically nonexistent between them in those next few moments as she rode him, and then it disappeared for real as he unfastened her jeans and shoved the material down her hips.

Strong fingers found her hot slit and she gasped. He inched deeper, opening her, pushing in, and a shudder ripped through her.

He shifted, moving and rubbing, working her as he caught her lips in a fierce kiss. His hand worked its magic, learning every secret as he plunged and played until she stiffened at the sudden rush of sweet sensation. A small cry ripped past her lips and a sizzling heat pulsed through her body as she grasped at the strong arms holding her tight. She floated for the next few seconds, the vibration of the music pounding the wall, keeping time with the throbbing in her body for a long moment before her eyelids finally fluttered open and she found him staring down at her, into her.

A rush of panic went through her and she turned,

putting her back to him, desperate to understand the sudden fear, to escape it.

"Don't," he murmured, the one word shredding what was left of her resistance. "Don't turn away."

"I'm not. I'm making things more interesting." She pressed her bottom against him in blatant invitation, and he was more than happy to oblige.

Strong fingers worked at the button on his jeans and then she felt the sag of denim. His erection sprang forward, hard and greedy, pushing against her for a split second before he pulled away.

"I need a condom," he murmured, his voice yanking her back to reality for a split second.

Her breath caught, her body blazing, as he retrieved a condom and worked it on with a speed that said he knew his way around the bedroom, and every other place she could possibly imagine. Because he wasn't some nice guy. He was as bad as they came. Dangerous.

The realization stirred a ripple of excitement, followed by another jolt of fear.

One that quickly drowned in a wave of heat as she felt the brush of knuckles against her backside as he positioned himself. His thick head nudged apart her slick folds and pressed into her just a fraction.

She closed her eyes against the slight pressure and caught her bottom lip. The pressure was so sweet as he stretched and filled her inch by decadent inch.

Slowly.

As if he knew just where to touch her and for how long. As if he knew her.

Her wants. Her desires. Her fears.

That her hopes and dreams were futile. That she would never be anything more than a wild child Tucker. That she didn't want to be.

The notion struck and the word was out before she could stop it. "Harder," she breathed, and he quickly obliged.

He filled her completely and her heart paused. The air lodged in her throat and her body throbbed, contracting around him, holding tight as if she never meant to let go. A tremor went through her and she fought to control the heat slip-sliding along her nerve endings, threatening her sanity and her control.

The hard tin vibrated against her fingertips, reminding her that she wasn't just spiraling out of control. She was doing it far from the safety of four walls. Reality crept in, along with the sounds drifting from inside the honky-tonk. The music and the laughter and the voices.

The notion sent a burst of excitement through her and she stiffened.

"We can't—"

"We are," Hunter's deep voice slid into her ears as his cock slid into her wet heat.

She closed her eyes, relishing the sensation all of five seconds before she heard a man's unfamiliar voice.

Just follow me, darlin', and we'll head back to my place."

Jenna felt Hunter's muscles tense. Her eyes opened and her head snapped up in time to see the couple that stumbled around the side of the building and headed for the row of cars parked near the treeline out back.

"Screw that," the woman murmured. "The backseat is just fine by me."

Jenna held her breath as gravel crunched and metal creaked. The door slammed, but the voices still carried through the open car window.

And while Jenna couldn't see anything thanks to a nearby dumpster that blocked the view, she could still hear them, which meant they could hear her.

The panting.

The moaning.

And damned if the notion didn't excite her more than it should have considering she'd turned over a new life and given up her old wild and wicked ways.

The realization zapped her like a lightning bolt and she tried to pull away, but Hunter was there, surrounding her, filling her up, his voice as stirring as it was soothing. "You're not scared of an audience, are you?"

"Who? Me?" She swallowed against her suddenly dry throat. "Of course not." At least she'd never been scared before. She was bold, wild, *bad*.

But he wasn't.

That's what she kept telling herself despite his every touch which proved otherwise.

"I was just thinking that you might not be comfortable with this. You *are* the sheriff."

"Yeah," he murmured, but her words didn't seem to slow him down in the least. One hand slid up her abdomen to her breast and he caught her nipple. He pinched the ripe tip until a burst of heat zapped her brain.

Her lips parted on a gasp. "I . . . I wouldn't want someone to hear us. For your sake."

"Don't worry about me, sugar. I can handle myself."

He slid his left arm around her, his fingers skimming her rib cage as he caught her other nipple. Now both hands plucked and rolled the sensitive tips until her knees went weak. "But if you want me to stop . . ."

"Yes," she managed a split second before he thrust into her. Still she caught the cry that curled up her throat and clamped her mouth shut as he started to move. "I mean, we really should."

In and out. Back and forth.

"Now," she added, but she didn't pull away or tense up. Instead, she pressed herself against him and arched against his delicious touch.

The backseat action going on nearby soon faded into the beat of her own heart as she drew him deeper, held him longer. The seconds ticked by as the pressure between her legs built. Tighter and tighter. Until every muscle went taut and just like that, she started to unwind. Sensation drenched her and she exploded around him. Her head fell back into the curve of his neck and a groan worked its way up her throat.

Before she could bite her lip against the sound, his mouth covered hers as he moved faster and plunged harder, deeper, stronger. Convulsions gripped him. She milked him, her slick folds clenching around his throbbing penis until a growl sizzled across her nerve endings.

He buried himself one last time and leaned into her. The rough wall rasped her overly sensitive nipples and desire speared her again. Every nerve in her body sizzled. She closed her eyes, relishing the aftershocks of her release, which swept through her and kept the fear at bay for the next several moments. Until reality washed back in and she became aware of the jeans down around her ankles. The warm night air slithered over her bare skin and a car engine grumbled nearby.

Close.

So close.

So what?

The notion struck and she stiffened.

"I really need to go," she blurted. "It's getting late and I have inoculations tomorrow at the Garber farm." She ducked underneath the arm to her left and put a few safe inches between them as she struggled with her clothes. "I, that is, it was nice. Thanks." And then she walked away because the last thing she needed was for Hunter DeMassi to see the gratitude blazing in her eyes. The wonder. The damned *happiness*.

Because Jenna Tucker had had her first decent orgasm in a long, *long* time. And her second. And they'd both been fantastic.

Not mediocre. Or decent. Or *nice*.

But fan-freaking-tastic.

Of all the rotten luck.

CHAPTER 24

A super-spectacular orgasm was good.

Jenna came to that conclusion after a night spent tossing and turning and damning her bad luck.

She'd always been a half-full kind of girl and the more she thought about it, the more she refused to worry over what had happened with Hunter.

Sure, it had caught her off guard. He wasn't an *it* type of guy and so she hadn't been ready for the wow factor.

But obviously he was an *it* guy in sheep's clothing. That could be a good thing. She had an itch that she needed to scratch and who better to do it with the wrong type of guy—a total badass—disguised as the right type of guy—Mr. Nice and Forgettable?

She had no intention of flaunting a sexual relationship with Hunter DeMassi. But it wouldn't exactly spell disaster for her newfound reputation if someone saw them together and thought they were dating.

Yes, this entire situation might be a blessing in disguise. She could beef up her good-girl image by dating the most well-respected man in town, and burn off her lust behind closed doors. It was a win-win.

Provided Hunter felt the same way.

Doubt niggled at her, pushing and pulling at the confidence that she'd worn for so many years. She tamped down on the unfamiliar feeling and gathered her courage.

There was only one way to find out.

"Can I help you?" Marge Sawyer Laraby was in her midsixties. She had thinning gray hair that was cut in a short bob and way too much green eye shadow. One carefully drawn-on eyebrow arched as she stared up from the front desk at the police station.

"I'm looking for the sheriff."

"Is that so?" The eyebrow arched even higher. "Police emergency?"

"No, no. It's more personal."

Marge opened her mouth to ask another question, but Hunter rounded the corner at that moment, a cup of coffee in one hand and a case file in the other. He looked a far cry from the hunky guy who'd seduced her last night and taken her over the top in the back parking lot of the honky-tonk. A sliver of disappointment rolled through her, followed by a rush of apprehension.

But then she caught the gleam in his eyes and her stomach hollowed out. Excitement chased up her spine and she knew that she'd definitely met her wolf in sheep's clothing.

"Can we talk?" she blurted. When Marge rested a hand on her chin, her ears perked, Jenna added, "In private?"

"Sure thing." He motioned her forward and she found herself following him down a small hallway. When they were safely inside his office, he sank down behind the desk and motioned her into a chair. "What's wrong?"

"Nothing." She shook her head. "That is, everything." Her gaze caught and held his. "It's about last night."

"It shouldn't have happened," he said before she'd had a chance to open her mouth again.

"Really?" She licked her lips. "I mean, is that what you really think? Because I was actually thinking that maybe it was a good thing that it happened because it got me thinking."

"About?"

"About doing it again."

"I thought you didn't do relationships?"

"I don't. It's just . . ." She licked her suddenly dry lips. "I'm not after a relationship." For the first time in her life, she found herself hesitating. She, Jenna Tucker, who'd never backed down from anyone or anything was actually floundering for her words.

Maybe she was changing, after all.

The notion bothered her even more than her sudden loss for words.

She shook the notion away and focused on the gleam in his eye and the heat rippling between them. "I've been thinking about last night. About what happened and what we should do about it now."

His eyes darkened, but he didn't reach out. Instead, he simply watched her. Waiting.

"I think we should do it again," she blurted. "And again. However many times it takes."

"For what?"

"For me to stop thinking about you. To forget." That's what this was really about. Deep in her gut, she'd convinced herself that Hunter would be like all the others. Nice and forgettable.

Only she wasn't forgetting.

Not yet.

"Make no mistake, I'm not after a relationship. This is purely physical. You're like a great dip that you can't stop eating. Eventually you take a bite and you don't want another."

"Is that so?"

A girl could hope. "I think the attraction's new and I've been depriving myself lately because, well, I'm trying to change my life and my image."

"So you're horny? That's what this is all about?"

"Yes. I mean, no. I mean, I'm thinking that maybe you're horny, too, and since we both are, maybe we could come to a mutually satisfactory agreement."

"Your cheeks are flushed," he noted, stepping closer. "And your pulse is erratic." He pressed a fingertip to the side of her neck in a slow, sweeping gesture that sent goose bumps chasing up and down her arms. "And you look a little faint. Do you always get faint when you get horny?"

No. She'd never once felt faint around any man. Even the hot guys she'd dated before her nice guy spell.

"You're turned on right now," he added. "Right here."

And how. Despite the fact that she'd cut loose last night, she was no closer to being free of the fantasies that haunted her night after night. If anything, she was even more worked up. Desperate. Hungry.

"What about you?" she countered. "Are you turned on?"

She didn't have to ask. She saw the blaze in his eyes, the tensing of his muscles, and felt the heat rolling off his body.

"I could go for round two."

Not that they were going another round right here and now.

She might be feeling some of the old Jenna feelings, but she wasn't the old Jenna. She wasn't going to strip off her clothes and throw herself across his desk.

"Okay, so we're both on the same page." She drew a deep, shaky breath. "We'll have sex again."

"And again."

Her gaze met his and a ripple of excitement went through her. "But no one can know. I mean, this is just temporary. I need a little action and you need a little action, but neither of us is looking for anything permanent, right? No relationship?"

He nodded and a whisper of regret went through her. A crazy feeling because Hunter DeMassi was the last person she wanted to get serious with. Sure, he turned her on in a major way now, but that would fade. It always did with guys like him.

She licked her lips and trembled at the anticipation that rippled through her. "Okay, great. We're both on the same page." She swallowed against her suddenly dry throat. "So, um, when should we start? You could stop by tonight after work. I've got to make a house call at the Miller farm, but I'll be home by six."

He looked as if he wanted to protest, but then Marge's

voice drifted over the intercom. "Sheriff, you've got a call on line one. It's Lorelei. She said Gerald's headed to the police station to pay Haywood a visit."

"Tell her I've got it on this end. Duty calls," he told her and she didn't miss the glimmer of regret. He pushed to his feet. "I need to catch Gerald before he does any damage to himself or anyone else."

"I'm surprised he can get around, what with his foot missing."

"He's not missing a foot."

"I heard that his foot was blown off."

"That's crazy. He suffered a wound to his big toe. A few stitches at best."

"What about his jaw? Is that still intact?"

"What are you talking about?"

She shook her head and gave him the lowdown on the gossip. "The joys of living in a small town," she finally said. "The stories just keep getting bigger and bigger." Which was why she needed to be careful with Hunter. She knew if anyone happened to see them together that they would be married with five kids by the time the news circulated. Or worse, the entire town would accuse her of corrupting the town's most respectable citizen.

Either spelled bad news for her future as a scandal-free businesswoman.

Then again, there were worse rumors. Married with kids was certainly a lot better than the rumor that she'd slept her way through the entire football team.

One lousy safety—and he had been lousy—and the next thing she'd known, she'd been walking around with Slut of the Century tattooed on her forehead.

Not that she'd cared. He'd ridden a motorcycle and

worn his hair a little too long and the idea of him—no matter how disappointing the reality—had been more exciting than the boring day-to-day of her small town.

She'd been so desperate for an escape back then, for a few blessed moments of *wow,* that she'd actually *liked* making the good people of Rebel talk.

Just like James Harlin.

"Folks like to talk, so let 'em talk," her grandfather had said more times than she could count. "I can't stand the lot of 'em anyhow, so better they're talking about me than to me."

Jenna had always felt the same way.

Then.

"I should go."

He grinned, a slow tilt to his lips that made her stomach flutter. "I'll catch up to you later."

I'm counting on it.

She'd propositioned him.

The knowledge followed Hunter throughout the rest of the day as he intercepted Gerald before the man had a chance to pull out his shotgun and blow off a few limbs, his own or anyone else's. He confiscated the gun and tossed Gerald into a holding cell until Lorelei could come and get him. A few more catastrophes involving the mayor's car getting towed and the cash register coming up short at McAbe's Mercantile, and Hunter managed to call it quits.

The sun was just setting when he pulled into the driveway at Jenna's place and climbed out of his truck.

"What do you say we take a little ride?" he asked when she opened the door wearing a pink sundress. Her feet were bare, her toes tipped in the same color as her dress.

She looked more sweet and wholesome than drop-dead sexy, but his body reacted the same. His gut twisted and his cock hardened, and it was all he could do not to reach out and touch her.

She was right. The deprivation was getting to him. He was way past horny and it was making him crazy.

Bat shit crazy.

"But I thought we could just hang out here," she started.

He shook his head. "If I do that, you're going to be flat on your back in the next five seconds."

Her grin was slow and deliberate. "I thought that was the idea."

He stiffened against the rush of heat whipping through his body. "We did that once. I want to draw it out this time." He needed to draw it out, to take his time and really enjoy himself.

That's why he still wanted her. Things had gone too fast and furious.

Not this time.

"Unless you like being stuck inside?" His question seemed to remind her of something and she glanced back at the sparsely furnished living room. Most of the furniture had been moved out to prepare for the demolition. Only an overstuffed chair and the console TV remained.

"Actually, I think I'd like to get out for a little while." The sadness slid from her gaze and excitement took its place. "Just let me get my shoes and I'll meet you at the truck."

CHAPTER 25

Jenna knew every makeout spot in town, but she had to admit that Hunter surprised her when he turned down a dusty back road that wound its way up and down several hills before winding to a stop at the edge of a rocky cliff.

She glanced through the windshield at the lake that shimmered in the moonlight below.

Rebel Lake had been a popular spot back in the day, but she'd never seen it from this angle.

"Please don't tell me we're trespassing on private property."

"This old road does cross the Benjamin spread, but since the old man died the place has been all but deserted. I've been keeping an eye on it for his daughter while she straightens out all the legal issues with the will. She's planning to put it up for sale as soon as the deed is transferred to her name."

"That's a shame. It's beautiful out here," she said as he swung the truck around and backed up to the edge of the cliff.

"Benjamin used to run cattle a long time ago, but he let the place go to hell after his wife died. There are a few head here and there, but mostly it's just lots of space and great views. I think the old man hoped his daughter and her husband would move back and run a few head. Maybe even buy some horses." He killed the engine, climbed out, and went to open up the back of the SUV.

"I can see this place running horses," she said as she followed him around to the back of the SUV.

The sharp drop-off overlooked a spectacular view of the canyon and the rippling water. The lake below had always been a hot spot for teens and several small bonfires blazed along the riverbank below. Ice chests lined the water's edge and Brantley Gilbert blasted from nearby truck speakers.

"I spent many a Saturday night down by that riverbank," she murmured.

"You and me both." He winked and settled on the back edge of the SUV. He patted the spot next to him. "But I think the view's a helluva lot better up here." She knew he was talking about the lake, but his gaze never left hers as he patted the seat next to him. "Hop up."

She hesitated, a crazy reaction because Jenna Tucker didn't hesitate when it came to men.

But this man was different.

He made her feel as if it were her first time settling down on the back of a tailgate, the moonlight overhead, the excitement zipping up and down her spine.

She climbed up and settled next to him.

He shifted his attention to the scene spread out before them. "I used to camp out at the lake back when I was bronc bustin'. We'd bring a couple cases of beer and unwind after a Saturday night ride. It's still just as pretty as ever. But then you've probably camped out down there a time or two."

"Or three." Her gaze followed the direction of his and she drank in the scene. A strange sense of longing went through her.

For the woman she'd once been.

The past she'd left behind.

The house that was this close to biting the dust in less than a few days.

She ignored the crazy thoughts. She was happy with the progress she was making. The changes.

They were good.

Great.

She focused on the frantic beat of her own heart and the six-foot-plus of warm, hard male sitting next to her. "I doubt you just sat by the water and drank beer with your buddies," she told him. "To hear tell it, you had quite the reputation yourself."

"Surely you know better than to believe everything you hear."

"Am I wrong?"

"No. But times change. I changed."

"I wish you'd share your secret. I've been trying to walk the straight and narrow and, for the most part, I'm making progress, but you know what they say. You're always seventeen in your hometown."

"Be careful what you wish for."

"What's that supposed to mean?" She slid him a sideways glance.

He seemed as if he wanted to say something, but then he shook his head. "You're right. I didn't spend most of my time down by the lake just drinking beer."

"Or enjoying the view."

A grin tugged at his lips. "Oh, I enjoyed it plenty. It just didn't have much to do with the water. Thirsty?" His deep voice slid into her ears and distracted her from the dangerous path her thoughts were taking.

She nodded. The SUV rocked as he slid off the tailgate to retrieve a small Yeti cooler from the front seat.

She drew several deep breaths and damned herself for not insisting they stay at her place. At the same time, she couldn't deny that he had a point. Last night had been fast and furious and much too fleeting. Maybe they did need to take their time and ease into things. Enjoy the moment. Milk it for all it was worth.

The notion sent a burst of excitement through her, almost as fierce as what she felt when he actually touched her. Her body tingled. Her nipples jumped to attention. A blazing heat swept her nerve endings and made it suddenly hard to breathe.

"It's awful hot." His deep voice drew her attention as he walked back, two beers in hand.

She took the bottle he offered her and held tight to the ice-cold brew. The icy condensation was a welcome relief against her blazing hot skin.

He hefted himself back onto the tailgate. Metal shifted and rocked and his thigh brushed hers.

A shock wave traveled across her nerve endings and made her hands tremble. She tightened her grip on the glass bottle and let the coldness sink into her skin.

Laughter drifted from below, the sound drawing her back to the past, to the many nights she'd spent with friends and the long list of bad boys who'd colored her reputation.

Funny, but at that moment she couldn't recall one face. They blurred in comparison to the tall, dark man that sat next to her, his blue eyes reflecting moonlight.

She took a pull on her beer and stared at the scene before her, her mind completely aware of the man sitting only inches away. As anxious as she was to get down to business, there was something oddly comforting about the silence that stretched between them, around them, twining tighter, pulling them closer. As if they were old friends who'd shared this exact moment time and time again.

As if.

Even so, a strange sense of camaraderie settled between them as they sat there for the next few moments. She sipped her beer while he downed the rest of his. One last swig and he set the bottle between them. It clinked and toppled onto its side, and she couldn't help herself.

"Did you ever play Truth or Dare?"

"I did a lot of things back in the day."

"What's that supposed to mean?"

"That sometimes it's a lot less work living up to people's expectations than it is changing their minds." He gave her a pointed look. "But then Sawyers don't take the easy way out. That's what my Mimi always told me."

"Neither do Tuckers. That's what James Harlin always told me. Then again, what he said and what he did were two very different things. I'd say he definitely took the easy way out."

"He didn't blow himself up on purpose."

"Didn't he?" She shrugged, that night rushing back into her mind until she could all but smell the smoke and hear the sirens. "He'd been working with that still too long to get sloppy. That explosion wouldn't have happened unless he wanted it to."

"It was an accident."

"Was it?" She voiced the one question that still haunted her. He'd always been so careful. No matter how drunk. How belligerent. He'd been different when it came to his shine. Methodical. "I can't help but think that maybe he just gave up. Everybody gets tired of trying." Of living up to expectations. Or, in James Harlin's case, not living up to them. He'd been a big disappointment for the most part. Maybe that truth had finally gotten to him. "Maybe he blew himself up on purpose."

"I don't know what was going through his mind that night," Hunter murmured, "but I do know that he didn't do it on purpose. Something was off."

"Is that why you haven't officially closed the investigation?"

He nodded. "The pieces just don't fit." And then he clamped his mouth shut on the subject as if words couldn't begin to explain his suspicions. "There's nothing specific. Just a feeling that there's more to it."

"A cop's hunch?"

"Something like that. Listen, I'm really sorry about what happened. I know it was hard on you and your sisters."

"We were used to being on our own." What she wasn't used to was the crazy emptiness that now sat inside her. The knowledge that her granddad was gone and never coming back. She'd been too young to feel the loss with her parents, but James Harlin . . . "I never thought I'd miss the old guy." She stiffened. "I shouldn't miss him."

"Yeah, well, what we should do and what actually happens are two different things."

"What do you mean?"

"I shouldn't miss my brother. It's not like we were close. We were always at odds. My dad pitted us against each other. It was always a contest, right up until the day I left. If you had asked me back then if I thought I would ever miss my brother, I would have said no. Hell, I would have thought it would be a relief not to have him around. No more competition. No constantly trying to measure up." He stared out at the scene below. "But then he became this saint and the pressure was even worse. Be as good as Travis. As upstanding. As respectable."

"I'd say you're measuring up just fine."

"I'm holding my own," he said after a long moment, as if hearing her say the words reaffirmed something deep inside. "So are you. You're growing up, Jenna Tucker."

"Because I'm not running around with every man that smiles my way?"

"Because you're reaching for something more."

"I don't know if I'll ever get there. The closer I get, the farther away that horse farm feels. And even if I do get it up and running, I'm not so sure I'll have enough business to stay in business."

"So?"

"So it all seems so futile sometimes."

"Maybe, but you reach for it anyway. You can't let your fears stop you. When I first ran for sheriff, the odds were not in my favor. But I did it anyway and look at me now, about to go for a third term."

"You don't sound all that excited." Something flashed in his gaze and she knew she'd touched on a sensitive subject. His look shuttered and she grasped for something to keep him talking, because as much as she wanted to get busy with Hunter DeMassi, she suddenly liked talking to him just as much. "How long has it been since you've ridden a bronc?"

"Over ten years."

"Don't you miss it?"

"Miss the aching shoulders and the cracked ribs?" He shook his head. "Picking yourself up after a hard throw is nothing but agony."

"So why did you do it in the first place?"

"Because the first few seconds were enough of a rush that it made the hurt worth it."

"And do you get the same rush from being sheriff?"

He shrugged. "Sometimes when I'm working a tough case. But not that many tough cases cross my desk in a small town like Rebel. For the most part, it's pretty calm. Tame."

Exactly what she wanted for herself. Or so she thought.

But seeing the flash of longing in his gaze, for another time and another place, another rush of excitement made her think that maybe, just maybe, walking the straight and narrow wasn't all she'd built it up to be.

"Tame is good," she heard herself say, but she no more believed it than he did at that moment.

There was just something almost sad about the look in his gaze and before she could stop herself, she slid off the tailgate and pulled him to his feet.

"What are you doing?"

"Trying to liven things up."

"I thought you said tame was good."

"I lied." Before he could say a word, she stood directly in front of him and nudged his knees apart.

Anticipation rippled through her as she leaned up on her tiptoes and leaned in close. His warm breath tickled her bottom lip and her mouth opened.

"Are you going to kiss me again?"

"Only if you don't start kissing me first," she murmured a split second before her mouth touched his.

The kiss was soft and sweet at first, but then he slid off the tailgate in front of her, pulled her close, and suddenly it was raging hotter than a forest fire.

He held her close and explored her mouth with his own, touching and tasting and taking her breath away until she clung to him for a long moment. And then he lifted her, sitting her on the tailgate and stepping between her legs to get closer for those next few breath-stealing moments.

The cold metal of the SUV bed met her back when he urged her back down, leaning over her, their lips still pressed together, tongues still tangled.

He pulled back, leaving her panting and staring up at him as he reached for the hem of her dress. He pushed it up her thigh, his gaze locked with hers.

"I guess we're getting to the good stuff now," she

murmured even though the past few minutes talking had been pretty nice, too.

"Oh, it's going to get good, all right." He continued pushing her dress up her leg, his fingers grazing her supersensitive skin. "Great, in fact."

The sultry promise chased the oxygen from her lungs as he urged her legs apart and wedged himself between her knees. His fingertips swept from her calves, up the outside of her knees until his hands came to rest on her thighs.

He touched his mouth to the inside of her thigh just a few inches shy of her panties. He nibbled and licked and worked his way slowly toward the heart of her. She found herself opening her legs even wider, begging him closer, eager for the bliss he'd shown her that night on the porch swing.

But this seemed different somehow. More intimate.

She wasn't sure if it was because they'd talked for those few minutes, but she felt closer to him somehow. *Connected.*

He trailed his tongue over the silk covering her wet heat and pushed the material into her slit until her flesh plumped on either side. She was so wet and he seemed to relish the discovery, tasting her sweetness as if she were a fine wine. He licked and nibbled at her until her entire body wound so tight she thought she would shatter at any moment.

She didn't.

She couldn't.

Not until she felt him flush against her body with no barriers between them. No clothing. No fear. No secrets.

Crazy.

There were plenty of secrets still left between them. Plenty of walls firmly in place.

She held tight to the thought and focused on the large hands gripping her panties.

She lifted her hips to accommodate him. The satin material slithered down her legs and landed on the trunk bed next to her.

He caught her thighs and pulled her toward the end of the tailgate, until her bottom was just shy of the edge. Grabbing her ankles, he urged her knees over his shoulders.

He slid his large hands beneath her buttocks and tilted her just enough. Dipping his head, he flicked his tongue along the seam between her slick folds in a long, slow lick that sent a moan bursting from her lips.

His tongue parted her and he lapped at her sensitive clit. He tasted and savored, his tongue stroking, plunging, driving her mindless until she knew she couldn't hold out any longer. Her cry shattered the darkness around them, mingling with the sounds that drifted from the riverbank below.

Her heart beat a frantic pace for the next few moments as she tried to come to terms with what had just happened.

She'd had the mother of all orgasms. An orgasm worthy of the most erotic dream.

But as satisfied as she felt, it still wasn't enough.

She opened her eyes to find him staring at her. A fierce look gleamed in his bright blue eyes, one that said he never meant to let her go, and a spurt of warmth went through her.

Followed by a rush of panic because there was no truth to any of it. The heat of the moment. The frenzied thoughts sparked by a good orgasm. This wasn't the beginning of anything permanent. It was all purely temporary. A fleeting moment in her life that she would remember fondly on all the lonely nights to follow.

That's why she'd agreed to this in the first place. A few days of lust and then they both walked away. She kept walking the straight and narrow, and so did he.

My turn.

That's what she wanted to say, but she wouldn't. While she'd agreed to indulge her lust for him, she had no intention of unleashing the bad girl that she'd locked down deep. Giving in to him was one thing, but turning the tables and taking charge?

Not happening.

Not yet.

The notion whispered through her and she stiffened.

"Stand up," he murmured, killing the push/pull of emotion inside of her and she quickly obliged.

She slid to her feet to stand in front of him. Her dress fell back down her thighs, covering the fact that her panties still hung on the edge of his tailgate.

A fact he was all too aware of if the tense set to his jaw was any indication.

He stood in front of her, his eyes gleaming in the growing shadows that surrounded them. His muscles bunched beneath his T-shirt. Taut lines carved his face, making him seem harsh, fierce, *hungry*.

She knew the feeling.

She swallowed against the sudden hollowness in her throat and fought to keep from reaching for the left strap of her sundress. But then he murmured "Undress," and she quickly obliged.

She slid one strap free, then the next, until the soft cotton material slid down her chest, her waist, her thighs, to pool at her feet. She reached for her bra next, her fingers going to the front clasp.

A quick flick and the cups fell away.

His gaze darkened and his nostrils flared, as if he couldn't get enough oxygen.

Her lips parted as she tried to drag some much-needed air into her own lungs. Her breasts heaved and his eyes shimmered.

"Damn, but you're something else, Jenna." The words were reverent and for a brief moment, she forgot all about the future and the past—everything save this moment and the urges building inside of her.

"I want to see you," she murmured.

"Soon, but you're still not done yet." His deep voice slithered into her ears and amped up her heartbeat.

"I don't have any clothes left."

"I do. Take them off."

She stepped forward to grasp the edges of his shirt. Flesh grazed flesh as she obliged him, pushing the material over his shoulders, down his arms, until it fell away and joined her discarded clothes. A brief hesitation and she reached for the waistband of his jeans.

A groan rumbled from his throat as her fingertips trailed over the denim-covered bulge. She paused, playing over and over the rock-hard erection until she couldn't stand it a moment longer. She wanted to feel the real thing in her hands. Working the zipper down, she tugged and pulled until the teeth finally parted. The jeans sagged on his hips. His cock sprang hot and pulsing into her hands.

She traced the ripe purple head before sliding her hand down his length, stroking, exploring. His dark flesh throbbed against her palm and her own body shuddered in response. She licked her lips and fought the urge to drop to her knees and taste him.

Luckily, he wasn't nearly as restrained.

He drew her to him and kissed her roughly, his tongue delving deep over and over until the ground seemed to tilt. And then he swept her up, laid her on the tailgate, spread her legs and sank hilt-deep inside.

CHAPTER 26

She still had her panties.

Jenna held tight to the knowledge as she slipped inside her house later that night. As wild and out of control as she'd been tonight, she'd had the good sense to grab her undies off his tailgate and stuff them into her purse. The steady hum of a motor out front reminded her that Hunter still hadn't pulled away yet and for a split second, she forgot her good fortune and thought about hauling open the door and doing a striptease for him in the blaze of headlights.

Despite the fact that she had to crawl out of bed before the crack of dawn in order to make it out to the Holiday Hills Ranch to take a look at their new breeding stock of goats the next morning.

The urge gripped her and her hands trembled, but then Jez scrambled from the kitchen. Her claws slid across the hardwood floor in a frantic scrape as she rushed for the door.

Jenna fought her lust and scooped up the white ball of fluff. The dog licked at her frantically for a few seconds before her high-pitched barks filled the air. Jenna set her on the floor and she danced in place for a few seconds before leading the way to the kitchen and the treat jar.

She gathered her control, forced herself away from the front door, and followed Jez into the kitchen. She unearthed the dog's favorite biscuits from the cabinet and fed one to the frantic animal.

The dog wolfed down the goodie and barked and danced for another.

"One a day. You know the rule."

Rules.

That's what her life was all about now. About respecting boundaries and walking the straight and narrow and playing it safe even if she had backslid for those few moments on the swing. And at the honky-tonk. And tonight overlooking the lake.

But she was home now.

Back to reality.

She walked into her bedroom and sank down on the bed. Eyeing the stack of letters, she thought about picking them up and continuing on with the story. Clara had already left for Chicago. The baby was due any day and she was planning how she was going to escape after the birth and get back to Texas, to her one true love, with their baby in tow.

Dearest P.J. was waiting and Clara was determined.

Even so, she'd obviously failed.

Clara was most certainly here in Rebel, so she'd made it back. She'd obviously been single upon her return because she'd gone on to marry a DeMassi and give birth to his son. A son who'd gone on to marry and have his own sons, one of which was Hunter's father.

There'd never been any whisperings of a scandal, no

illegitimate child haunting Clara and her family. Jenna knew that firsthand because she'd inadvertently milked Miss Ann at the clinic for information.

"Can you believe Clara Bell Sawyer is going to be ninety-three? I can't imagine living that long," she'd said earlier that afternoon while handing over a stack of charts to be filed.

"Well the Lord certainly blesses those who do his work," Miss Ann had said, taking the files and handing Jenna her next chart—a python by the name of Monty who had stopped eating his usual diet of mice after downing a plastic fern from his aquarium. He was stopped up and it was Jenna's job to act as the plunger. "Clara Bell has always been a treasure to this town. A shining example of a fine woman. She married well and had a fine family. Our very own sheriff is proof of that, although I hear tell he was certainly a wild one back in the day. Might have thrown it all away on that rodeo nonsense if it hadn't been for Clara's guidance. She kept him on the up and up and now he's carrying on the family tradition and doing the Sawyers proud."

Even if his own parents didn't realize it.

She remembered Hunter's earlier comments about his brother and his folks. They never called.

Or cared.

She couldn't imagine abandoning her own child.

Any more than Clara could imagine giving hers up for adoption.

But she'd obviously done it.

The notion stirred a rush of sadness and Jenna bypassed the letters and killed the light. The truth would come soon enough, just as tomorrow would dawn and she would be back to work, walking the straight and narrow and trying not to think about Hunter and the next time she would see him.

For now, she wanted to hold the moment. The satisfaction. The hope.

Just for a little while longer.

Hunter watched the bedroom window go dark before he shoved the truck into Reverse and pulled out of Jenna's drive all the while fighting the urge to haul ass up her front steps, pull her out onto the porch, and take her up against the front of the house. Her back flat against the peeling wood. His thigh pressing between her legs. His hands pulling at her clothes. Her hands clutching his back. His cock pushing deep into her wet heat . . .

He stiffened against the urges and his fingers tightened on the steering wheel.

Drive, a voice screamed. *Now. Before you lose the head on your shoulders and start thinking with the one between your legs.*

Not because he cared if someone happened along and saw them together.

This wasn't about Jenna and her worry that someone might see them together and get the wrong idea.

He was worried about his own sense of self-preservation. She made him want to do things that no fine, upstanding man should want to do. She brought out the bad ass in him that he'd fought so long to deny.

Too long.

He wasn't going back to the man he'd once been. Not for Jenna or anyone else.

He'd made a life for himself. One built on respect and

admiration and acceptance—all the things he'd never had growing up.

Things he'd never deserved.

Until now.

He was the sheriff, for Christ's sake. He had a career. A flawless reputation. He certainly wasn't giving it all up for a good lay.

Even a phenomenal one.

Jenna Tucker was just a temporary fall from grace. A rush of excitement to tide him over during all the long, boring nights to come.

He certainly wasn't falling for *her*.

Not no, but *hell* no.

CHAPTER 27

". . . go for bachelor number one, I tell ya. Number one!"

Kim Bowman heard the familiar voice drifting from her apartment the minute she reached the second-floor landing. Anyone else who lived alone might have reached for their cell and dialed 911 to report an intruder. But Kim wasn't just the youngest resident among the over-sixty set that inhabited the Rodeo Street apartment complex, the first of its kind in small-town Rebel, Texas. With two stories, a pool, and a hot tub, it was the latest in well-developed living. The only thing in town that came even close was the senior center. But the pool was therapeutic and the hot tub strictly for arthritic patients, so the Rodeo Street complex won hands down when it came to luxury and had, in fact, become the hot spot for those aging seniors who weren't ready for twenty-four-hour care and supervision.

Which meant she was the only one on the second floor with cable TV because most of her neighbors either a) couldn't afford it, or b) thought it was the work of communist Hollywood trying to spread their propaganda and take over the world.

While Kim subscribed primarily for Animal Planet,

she also received everything from the Golf Channel to the twenty-four-hour Game Show Network—a favorite of her next-door neighbor and resident handyman, Elijah Lucretious Camper.

"Hi, Mr. Camper," she said as she pushed open the door to find the seventysomething man parked on one end of her beige sofa. A rerun of *The Dating Game* blazed on her TV. A half-empty bowl of granola sat on her coffee table next to a large wrench and her remote control.

"Hey there, little lady." He grabbed a handful of granola, popped it into his mouth, and pushed to his feet. His face puckered as he chewed. "How can you eat this stuff?"

"Granola is healthy."

"And tasteless. I got two words for you: pork rinds. Now there's a snack with some bite."

"I'll remember that the next time I'm in the health food aisle at the Piggly Wiggly. So what are you doing here so late?"

He retrieved his wrench and motioned to the kitchen. "Just changing that S-pipe under your sink."

Since Kim had had the cable hooked up, her apartment had skyrocketed to the top of Mr. Camper's maintenance list. If it wasn't her S-pipe, it was her leaky toilet or a strange humming in her refrigerator, or the invisible mouse he still hadn't been able to catch, despite his best efforts. Just last Saturday, he'd shown up with a *TV Guide,* a six-pack of root beer, and three cans of Cheez Whiz, the last of which he'd sworn would nab the little bugger. But after three hours and six episodes of *Wheel of Fortune,* he still hadn't caught the rodent.

Not that there was one. The mouse, along with all the other repairs, were Mr. Camper's excuses to watch her cable TV.

"I hate to keep you up so late. The sink could have waited until tomorrow."

"No trouble." He shrugged. "I just got my second wind."

She smiled. "Just in time for *The Dating Game,* I see." His favorite, though he enjoyed everything from *Wheel of Fortune* to *The Price Is Right. And of course, a few episodes of* Jeopardy *here and there, or* Who Wants to Be a Millionaire? *didn't hurt either.*

"They got celebrity guest reruns on tonight." His gaze shifted to the TV where a platinum blonde was capering about, dressed in go-go boots and brilliant blue eye shadow. "Why, that Pamela Anderson looks just like my Priscilla did back then. Man, but she was a looker." Priscilla was the late Mrs. Camper. She'd died of heart failure more than ten years ago, and she was one of the main reasons Kim put up with Mr. Camper and his game shows. Not that she'd been personally acquainted with Priscilla. The woman had long since passed on by the time Kim had buried her own mother and moved into the Rodeo Street apartment. But whenever the old man mentioned his dearly departed wife, a soft, lovesick expression flashed in his eyes.

That, and a look of overpowering loneliness.

While Kim wasn't the least bit familiar with the first emotion, loneliness she knew all too well.

"She certainly is pretty." Kim left her laptop bag by the door, along with a few extra leads and collars she'd picked up in the barn after the students had forgotten them, and kicked off her boots.

"And stubborn." He frowned as he watched Pam make her decision. "If I said it once, I said it a dozen times. Number one." He punched the Off button on the remote and went to retrieve his toolbox from the kitchen. "So why were you out so late?"

"I got stuck working late on my lesson plans for next year." She followed him out to the kitchen and braced herself for the coming lecture.

"It ain't right for a young girl to be roaming the streets at this ungodly hour."

"I wasn't roaming the streets. I was at the school and then I came straight home."

"It's still an ungodly hour. Anything can happen. You got that Mace I picked up for you?"

"In my purse."

"What about the whistle?"

"I don't think I need—"

"Just 'cause this is a small town don't mean you can run around as bold as you please and not have to worry about any crazies. Why, we got plenty of 'em right here, I tell ya. I saw Myrna Lynn Vernon slap Sally Ferguson with a loaf of French bread in the bakery section of the grocery store just yesterday and all 'cause Sally tried to cut in line. People live by a thread these days, I tell ya. A thread that can snap at any time. That's why we got all this road rage now."

The closest thing to road rage that they had in Rebel had been an incident involving two high school baseball players who'd taken out a few mailboxes after celebrating a little too much after playoffs. Not that Kim was going to mention that and risk getting Mr. Camper started on the disgruntled youth of today.

". . . a girl's got to protect herself," he went on. "So what about the whistle?"

She indicated the nylon rope tied to her key chain and the small piece of metal that hung suspended.

"Good for you," he said and a small spiral of warmth went through her. Mr. Camper might be nuttier than a pan of pecan muffins, but he was also sweet and caring. He constantly nagged her about being cautious, but he also left the newspaper on her doorstep every morning, took out her trash, and had even programmed her DirecTV to record the stock show finals in Houston. The least she could do was let him borrow her TV to watch his nightly game shows.

"So the sink is fully functional now?" she asked, even though she'd made coffee and done dishes just that morning.

"That's how it looks, but don't be fooled by appearances." He tossed the wrench inside the toolbox sitting on her small, round kitchen table and slammed the lid shut. "It might look and run okay, but I've still got to put in a new seal." He held up a piece of black rubber. "This'll do away with that squeaky sound it's been making every time you hit the garbage disposal switch."

She turned on the switch. "I don't hear anything but grinding."

"Sure you do." He leaned in close to the stream of water for several seconds. "There. That's a squeak if I ever heard one."

"I just hear grinding."

"Don't fret." He went on as if she hadn't said a word. He flicked the switch off and gave her a sturdy look. "I'll get over here tomorrow night and get this puppy runnin' real nice and quiet."

She arched an eyebrow at him. "*Price Is Right* marathon?"

A grin crinkled his old face. "*Family Feud* is hosting famous reality TV families." He hefted his toolbox and started for the front door. "The Kardashians are going up against that one housewife from New Jersey and her bunch."

"Sounds like fun."

"All in a day's work, little gal. All in a day's work. Speaking of work, I won't be able to get over here next week on account of my grandson is coming into town. He's helping out one of the local ranches, helping them to go digital with computers and some such nonsense."

"So he's into computers?"

"Lives and breathes the blasted things. So don't go breaking anything while I'm busy."

"Sure thing," Kim murmured as she closed the door behind Mr. Camper. Her bones ached with exhaustion, but she wasn't nearly ready to call it a night and climb into bed. Instead, she retrieved her laptop. She needed to make a few changes to the lesson plan and e-mail one of the local FFA chapters about new guidelines for this year's stock show.

While the laptop was booting up, Kim grabbed her phone and tapped the Voice Mail icon.

"This is Katy. What do you think about teal? Jake likes teal but he doesn't have to wear it. You do. Call me."

While Kim loved her friend, she couldn't help but

envy her. Katy had found Jake living in the apartment below her in Austin. No dating apps. No swiping left or right. Just a knock on the door downstairs, and bam, instant life partner.

Beep.

"It's Katy again. What about lavender? Royal purple? It's an evening wedding, but we could go either way because I want you to be comfortable. To wear the dress again. I want to break the ugly bridesmaid's dress cycle. Call me."

Beep.

"Hi, Kim," Gabe's voice blasted over speakerphone. "Bad news. Can't make our karaoke date. Mom has laryngitis from doing too much Rhianna and she doesn't think she'll have her voice back in time. But how about dinner? Saturday night. Our place. Seven sharp."

Kim leaned her head back against the sofa, closed her eyes, and fought back a wave of despair.

So, he lived with his mother. So what? Living alone was not one of the *Redbook* requirements for a perfect husband. So long as the person he lived with wasn't a significant other.

Being ready to settle down was one of the requirements, which was why the dates with Benny had progressed to two, then three. They were holding steady at four with no commitment as of yet since she'd yet to rule out Gabe. But Kim knew that Benny wouldn't wait forever. He'd taken to playing Marvin Gaye's "Let's Get It On" whenever they were in his car.

While she liked his enthusiasm, she couldn't quite picture herself waking up to him every morning. Or going to bed with him. Or *being* in bed with him.

Not that sex had anything to do with anything. Sex could be misleading. People married all the time on the basis of great sex—marriages that usually ended in divorce because humping each other's brains out simply couldn't take up twenty-four hours of the day. People had to talk to each other, to interact, and in order to do so, they had to like each other.

Beep.

"What about hot pink? Do you like hot pink? It's Katy. Call me . . ."

Beep.

"I've got one word: camouflage. Mind you, it's not my suggestion. It's Jake's. He thinks we should change the theme to Duck Dynasty, but I wanted to get your opinion first. Call—" The message cut off as the phone rang.

Kim snatched up the receiver. "Please stop obsessing about this. It's not good for your nerves. I'll waltz down the aisle in a Pokemon T-shirt if that's what you want."

"Just the shirt? Or are we talking pants, too?" The deep, compelling voice rumbled over the line and a tingle swept the length of Kim's spine.

She sat up straighter. Heat rushed to her cheeks. "I— I'm sorry. I, um, thought you were someone else."

Laughter rumbled, so deep and soothing and stirring. "A lucky someone if we're talking just the T-shirt."

Her cheeks burned hotter. "No, no, she's just a friend. She's getting married and she's been stressing, trying to pick the right dress color even though I couldn't care less." Okay, so she was rambling on to a stranger. "By the way, who is this?"

"Carter Walls. I'm looking for my grandfather. I'm

here at his place, but he's not here. Your number was by the phone along with a *TV Guide*. He's not by chance watching TV up there, is he?"

"He was, but he left. You might check at apartment 16B."

"They have DirecTV?"

"Better. They've got peach fritters. Your granddad has a thing for old lady Maxwell's fritters."

"Is that what they're calling it these days?"

A smile tugged at her lips. "It's bunko night. She hosts every third week and makes her prize-winning fritters. If you don't have the number, you could probably just stop by. I'm sure old lady Maxwell won't mind."

"Thanks, I'll do that."

"No problem."

Silence settled for a few frantic heartbeats while Kim debated whether or not to hang up. "So," she blurted before common sense intervened. "You're in town early, huh?"

"I finished my last IT project a few days ahead of schedule. Thought I'd surprise Gramps. Listen, thanks for the info. I hope I didn't take you away from anything."

"Just work."

"That's no fun." The words slid into her ears and sent a rush of warmth through her body. "So what about it?"

"What about what?"

"You want to get together and do something fun?"

"But you've never even met me."

"My Gramps has told me about all about you. You're the Agriculture teacher. You're single and you spend way too much time on all those dating websites."

"So you're not swiping on Tinder, huh?"

"Hell, no. It's all about chemistry. You can't get that on a website. So what do you think? You want to go out?"

His soft chuckle whispered over her senses and her heart pounded faster.

Pounded? Holy moly, her heart *was* pounding. And she was tingling. And there was this heat . . .

"Kim?"

"Um, what?"

"What about it? Dinner? Tomorrow night?"

"I don't . . ." The words seemed to catch in her throat and she swallowed. "That is, we really shouldn't . . ." Her throat tightened again and damned if she could get the words out.

"If you're busy, we could try for a different night . . ."

"No, no. I'm not busy." Now why had she told him that? He'd given her an out, but she hadn't taken it.

Because she didn't want out. She wanted dinner.

"Why not?" she heard herself say.

It was just dinner. It wasn't like she had anything better to do. Like she was putting off the rest of her life to follow a whim. Gabe had canceled, after all. That meant sitting home, swiping prospects on her phone and listening to her own arteries harden because she was sure to reap the consequences of that extra large order of French fries she'd had at lunch.

A weak moment, but no more.

"But no BBQ," she added, determined to get back on her diet. "And nothing fried."

"That just about rules out all the food groups around here."

"Actually, I know this great little health food place."

What? She might be going against all common sense at the moment, acting on hormones rather than cool, calm logic, but she hadn't hitched a ride on the Crazy Train just yet.

She had her priorities straight, even if her heart was beating ninety to nothing.

CHAPTER 28

"What do you mean she's still in bed?" Hunter asked when Pam informed him that Mimi wasn't in the common room. "It's after lunch."

Pam shrugged. "She's not feeling well."

"Nonsense," came the voice from a nearby doorway.

He turned to see his Mimi wearing the pink robe he'd bought her for Christmas last year and a pair of matching slippers.

"What's wrong?" he asked.

"Why does everyone keep asking me that?" She grimaced. "I'm fine."

"You're wearing a robe," he pointed out. "You never wear a robe in the middle of the day."

"I wear this robe plenty. It's my favorite." She motioned to Pam.

"That's right," the woman agreed. "I see her in it all the time."

But she'd never worn it during one of his visits. Instead, she was always dressed in a pantsuit or a dress, her hair perfectly coiffed, her lipstick on and eyelashes in place.

"I'm fine." She waved another hand as if to say the subject was closed. "Now tell me you gave the slingshot subject a little more thought"—she motioned to the white bag in his hand—"and changed your mind about bringing me contraband."

"I'm afraid not. It's just a muffin," he said, holding up the bag. Because he'd done plenty of thinking the night before about all his great-grandmother had done for him. And all she asked in return? A slice of lemon loaf and a slingshot. Since he wasn't about to make it past the front desk and Beatrice Tucker, the dietician who monitored all of the food that came in via family members, he'd picked up a healthy alternative that couldn't be confiscated.

"The cookie didn't work. Stella Blankenship is allergic to peanuts and accused me of trying to send her into shock, which wouldn't have been a bad thing if I could have convinced her to take at least one measly bite. But Beatrice caught up to us and confiscated the blasted thing so I didn't even get a chance to stab her with the EpiPen." Clara waved a hand. "A muffin isn't going to work unless there are some nuts hidden in the center like a file in one of those cakes they sneak into a prison." Hope fueled her gaze. "There's no chance of that, is there?"

"The muffin isn't for her. It's for you."

"I'm not allergic."

"I know that. There are no peanuts in it. It's bran." Brandy Tucker had told him it was perfect for anyone on a restricted diet when he'd stopped by the bakery that morning. He'd been after a dozen of Jenna's favorite cupcakes. A gesture that had caused a raised eyebrow and a questioning look from Brandy Tucker McCall.

But in all honesty, he'd bought the cupcakes as a consolation gift because he wasn't going to see Jenna tonight. Or tomorrow night. Or any other night.

He was putting a stop to their arrangement before things got any more complicated.

Before Hunter DeMassi got in over his head to the point that he stopped thinking about the good of the town because he was too busy thinking about her. Wanting her.

Falling for her.

Hell, no.

The truth had hit him over the past few days as his thoughts had been more and more consumed by their after-hours activities, to the point that he'd almost blown his cover out at the still site. He'd been so busy thinking about Jenna that he'd almost missed a new camera that had been set up a few yards into the tree line. Proof that they were suspicious that someone was on to them.

He couldn't get careless again.

He had work to do. A town to run. His sanity to preserve.

"It's good for you," he added when Mimi stared at him as if he'd grown two heads. "It's low in sugar."

"What's the point of a muffin if it has to be good for you?" She glanced up. "I didn't stick around this long so that I could spend my glory years eating bran. How depressing is that?" she asked Pam.

"I think it's nice that he cares about you," the nurse

told Mimi. "You're lucky to have someone who loves you so much."

"I am, aren't I?" A smile touched her lips, along with a hint of sadness. "At the same time, there is such a thing as caring too much." A frown pulled her expression tight. "You spend too much time here. Don't you have anything better to do on a Sunday afternoon?"

"What's that supposed to mean?"

"Shouldn't you be at the church picnic?"

"I already put in an appearance, drank a glass of tea, and now I'm here."

"I'm not talking about keeping up appearances. I'm talking about living. You should be out living instead of babysitting a sick old woman."

"I'm not following you."

"You used to have so much life in you. Now you're just going through the motions."

"I used to be hell on wheels to quote you."

"Exactly." A smile touched her lips. "You were a handful back then. But then you had to go and grow up."

"That's a good thing, Mimi."

"Yes, I suppose it is. We all have to grow up sometime and let the past go." The sadness was back then. "Even if we don't want to."

"What's going on, Mimi?"

She didn't answer for a long moment as if lost in her own thoughts. But then she smiled and patted his hand. "It makes no nevermind. So tell me all the juicy gossip. Did Gerald have a penile implant? 'Cause that's what Maureen told Stella who told Janine. Said she heard it from Lorelei herself. Said everybody is saying that he wasn't discombobulated, but in actuality he was. Gerald just had a penile implant to repair everything so that Haywood wouldn't think he got the best of him."

"If the man had to have an implant then Haywood definitely got the best of him."

"So you're saying it's true."

"It's not true. It's ridiculous. I was just saying that a penile implant is not winning any war."

"Told you, Pam." Mimi glanced at the nurse. "No penile implant."

"That's a good thing."

"Yeah, yeah." Clara waved a hand. "Good for him, disappointing for the rest of us."

"You don't seriously like seeing the Tuckers and the Sawyers going at it all the time, do you?"

"It makes no difference what I like. It's a fact just like the sun rising and setting. That's one thing I've learned in all my years here. You can try all you want, but you can't change people. They are who they are. You can only change people's perceptions of you. Like you did."

"But I did change, Mimi."

A gleam touched her eyes. "Let's hope not. I think I'm ready for my nap." She turned to Pam before Hunter could ask her what she meant. "Take care," she told him.

"I'll see you next time."

She didn't answer and a strange sense of worry wriggled through him. "What's up with her?" he asked Pam after she'd signaled an orderly to take Mimi back to her room.

"I don't know. She woke up yesterday complaining that she was still tired. I called the doctor. He sent out some medication for her until he gets in for rounds tomorrow. He said it's probably just her age catching up to her. I should be so lucky as to be in that good of a shape when I'm ninety-two. If I ever get there."

"You and me both."

His Mimi was getting old. It made sense that she would start to slow down mentally as well as physically. Even say a few off-the-wall things.

"You used to have so much life in you. Now you're just going through the motions."

Like hell. He wasn't going through the motions. He was still living, all right. Living a better life than the one he'd had. He was making a contribution to the world. Doing some good. Paying it forward instead of stuck in a selfish rut just worried about his own happiness.

He'd spent far too long chasing the rush of a good ride, feeding his own need for excitement.

But the world didn't revolve around him and no way was he just going through the motions now.

His Mimi was wrong. Confused. Old.

He knew that.

So why did her words still bother him so damned much?

Clara's baby was dead.

Jenna sat on her grandfather's overstuffed plaid chair—the last piece of furniture still left in the house—and reread Clara's words of anguish and grief and blinked against the burning behind her eyes. Denial rushed through her and her heart all but stopped as she read the heartbreaking words . . .

. . . I held my beautiful baby girl for the first and the last time. I held her for hours even though they kept trying to

take her away from me. I prayed for her to open her eyes.
For her skin to pink up and warm to the touch. But my
prayers went unanswered. Like always. They finally took
her and left me with nothing but my self-loathing. She's
gone and I have only myself to blame because I couldn't
save her from the inevitable, just as I couldn't save you
from the hatred of an entire town . . .

Jenna folded the paper and stuffed it back inside the
envelope. There were still six more letters that she'd in-
tended to get through before finishing up the last of her
packing. Brody and his guys were anxious to get started
on the demolition. Something that should have happened
days ago, but she'd been too busy with work to empty
out what little remained in the house.

Too busy with the letters.

With Hunter.

She'd been stalling, putting off the inevitable just as
Clara had been when she'd held her baby and refused
to let go.

But Jenna was doing just that.

It didn't matter that the letters continued and there
were still a few odds and ends in the kitchen cabinets,
life had to go on. Clara's life, where it had seemed
more like an intriguing soap opera before, now seemed
more real this time. The pain palpable. Jenna knew that
she could no more keep reading than she could put off
the demolition of the house, or keep up the agreement
with Hunter. All three—the letters, the packing,
Hunter—had been a distraction from the reality of what
she was doing.

Evolving.

Changing.

Saying good-bye.

But things were getting too real now. The feelings too intense. Forget a distraction. All three were sucking her in, pulling her in different directions and she needed to get back on track.

It was time to let go of the letters.

The house.

Hunter.

Time to move on.

CHAPTER 29

"Miss Clara?" Jenna stood in the doorway of Room 5C at the senior living facility and eyed the frail woman lying on the bed.

She'd seen Clara Bell many times over the years. At the weekly church picnic. At the annual jalapeño festival. Out and about town with her senior shopping group.

But she'd never seen her like this.

"She's not feeling well," came the familiar voice behind her. Jenna turned to see her second cousin Pam. "I don't know if now is such a good time for a visit."

"I just came by to drop off something that belongs to her." Jenna fished out the stack of letters from her purse. She'd thought about giving them to Hunter, but they just seemed too personal and so she'd gone straight to the source. "If you could give them to her . . ."

"Who's that?" came the old woman's voice.

Jenna turned to see Clara Bell staring at her with familiar blue eyes.

Hunter's eyes.

"It's me. Jenna Tucker. I'm renovating my granddad's old house and I found something that I think belongs to you."

"Something of mine? At James Harlin's house?"

"It seems so." She waited for the old woman to say something negative. That's the way it always was with the older set in Rebel. They were still caught up in the feud that had torn the town apart so many years ago.

But Clara only smiled. "Well don't just stand there, girl. Bring it over here."

"I'll just leave you two," Pam said, motioning Jenna forward. She left then, closing the door behind her.

"I found these in an old trunk in the attic. They have your name on them." She handed over the pink letters and watched as recognition lit the old woman's eyes.

"Why, I haven't seen these in years." She took the letters with one frail hand and set them on the bed beside her. "I figured they got thrown away a long time ago."

"No, ma'am." Jenna licked her lips and tried not to think of Hunter with those same blue eyes.

Eyes that had looked into her and seen everything she'd fought so hard to hide from everyone. From herself.

"I read them," she said before she could stop herself. "Not all of them, but some. I didn't know what they were at first."

Clara Bell arched one silvery brow. "And then they got pretty juicy so it was hard to stop, right?"

"I didn't mean to pry."

"Don't you worry about that."

"I just want you to know, your secrets are safe with me. I won't tell anyone about the baby. Or P.J."

Regret lit her eyes and her hand tightened on the stack. "I appreciate that. It's hard to believe in such a small town that there are still secrets. But then people believe what they want to believe. When my daddy said Archibald Tucker betrayed him, everybody believed him. No questions asked. Their imagination was better than any answer Daddy would've given them. Still, it's hard to believe that nobody put two and two together, what with my running off to Chicago. But then P.J. was here making sure that no one suspected the truth. Even my daddy."

"I'm afraid I don't understand. Your daddy knew about P.J., right?"

"Of course he did. It's hard to ignore a man who steps up and takes responsibility for the bastard child growing in his daughter's belly. Daddy blamed P.J. and, therefore, Archibald. That's what caused the rift between them. Bless P.J. He was my one true friend. He gave up everything to save my name, even though he didn't have to."

"But he did have to, right? I mean, morally. He was the father, after all."

"P.J.?" She actually looked surprised before she gave a sad shake of her head. "Sweet girl, P.J. wasn't the father. He was my best friend. The father of my dear Bonnie was my high school Physics teacher." Her eyes gleamed. "I loved that man with all my heart. I never stopped loving him, even after I lost the baby. I came back home hoping to see him again, but he'd moved away." She shrugged her frail shoulders, her nightgown sliding off one shoulder just a fraction to reveal the pale translucent skin beneath. "It turns out he didn't love me as much as I loved him. Isn't that always the case?" She shook her head. "P.J. was a good friend, but I wasn't. I let him risk everything for me because I was willing to risk everything for the father of my child." She settled into a sad silence for a few moments before shaking her head. "But enough about my secrets." Her gaze grew hopeful. "Tell me some of yours."

"Excuse me?"

"Hear tell from Pam who heard from a friend of hers that you and my great-grandson were out dancing last Friday night."

"I . . . That is, we . . ." She licked her lips again, her mind racing now that Clara had turned the tables on her. "We didn't actually go together, but we did do a little dancing while we were there." In the back parking lot, that is.

"And?"

"And nothing. That's all it was. Just a few dances. But now it's over," she rushed on. "We're not really right for each other. Not enough for a relationship or anything like that." What the hell was she saying? Clara Bell hadn't said one word about a relationship so why did Jenna feel the need to explain? Because the old woman eyed her as if she knew exactly what was going on.

As if she could relate.

She could, Jenna realized as she sat there with Clara Bell Sawyer. The woman knew what it was like to fall for a man that was all wrong for her. And to suffer the consequences.

Hunter might look like the right man for Jenna on the surface, but beneath the uniform and the respect of an entire town, he was every bit the wild child he'd been back in the day.

He made her feel every bit the wild child she'd been. Then.

"I'm not interested in him and he's not interested in me," she added. "He's not my type and I'm not his."

"And that matters because . . . ?"

"Because it's a disaster waiting to happen." She was trying to alter the course of her life. To leave her old self behind. To change. She couldn't do that with a man who constantly reminded her of the woman she'd once been. A bad boy who called to the bad girl deep inside. "You know that."

"I do, don't I?" She shook her head. "Still, it's a shame."

"Excuse me?"

"For all the heartache, I wouldn't go back and change anything. I mean, I would. I wouldn't let P.J. step up and take the blame. That much I regret. I tore apart our families and I'm sorry for that. But I don't regret falling in love. Or having my baby. Those were the good parts. The high notes, so to speak. It's been downhill from there."

"I can't say that I'm following you."

"What I'm trying to say is Hunter's a good man. He deserves to have a little fun once in a while regardless of what the folks around here think." She sighed then, the sad, lonely sound of a woman who was really and truly tired of her life and everything in it. "I think I'd like to go back to my nap now. You run along. And if you see my great-grandson again, make sure he has a good time." She closed her eyes. "When you get old like me, the memories are all that you have left."

"Here you go." The owner of the hardware store handed over the short list of names to Hunter. "We sold exactly three of those locks in the past two years. Here are the folks who bought them."

Hunter took the paper as a wave of excitement rushed through him. This was it.

Sure, there was always the possibility that the lock had been bought somewhere else. A slim possibility since Bucky had informed him that he was the only authorized dealer of this particular type of lock for a two-hundred-mile radius. The odds were in Hunter's favor.

Even more, there was just something deep in his gut that told him he was *this* close to uncovering the truth and shutting down the entire operation.

A bust that would make him a shoo-in for the next election.

"Thanks, Bucky."

"Anytime, Sheriff." The man waved him off as Hunter headed out to his SUV.

Climbing behind the wheel, he texted the three names to Gator to see if he might know of a connection and then he called in to Marge to pull the address for the first name.

"Boris Miller? What do you want with that old coot?"

"Parking violation."

"But I didn't see anything in the file—"

"Just pull the address so I can go by and talk to him."

"Sure thing. Oh, and I stuck a blueberry muffin in your glove compartment. You need to keep up your strength."

"Thanks, Marge."

"Oh, and there was a call from the senior center while I was at lunch. You're supposed to stop by as soon as you get a chance."

"I'm not bringing Mimi a slingshot. You can tell her I said that."

"It wasn't Clara Bell. The call came from that nurse—Pam Tucker."

She's just calling to give you an update.

That's what he told himself. But he knew the minute he heard her name that something wasn't right. Mimi always called herself. If Pam was calling, that meant that Mimi couldn't. Which meant . . .

The thought rooted in his head, the worry, the fear, the truth.

He shoved the key into the ignition, gunned the engine and hauled ass down Main Street, headed for the Royal Rebel Arms.

CHAPTER 30

"I'm so sorry about Clara Bell," said the familiar female voice.

It was the same sentiment Hunter had heard over and over for the past few days since he'd arrived at the senior center to find that his Mimi had had a massive stroke and passed away.

He'd known the truth even before Pam had stared at him with that regretful look and told him he would have to talk to the doctor for a complete update on his great-grandmother's condition.

The update had amounted to a thirty-second explanation of how she'd been suffering a few ministrokes over the past few days, which had rendered her tired and listless and made her seem slightly off. The ministrokes had led up to the big one and now she was gone.

And Hunter was all alone.

"She was a fine woman," Myrtle Sinclair added. "One of the good ones."

"She was," Hunter agreed, shaking the woman's hand and turning to the next person passing in front of him. An endless stream of faces blocked his view of the casket as it was lowered into the ground at Sawyer Hill, a stretch of rolling green hills dotted with lush flowers and shrubs. The final resting place for the entire Sawyer clan. Clara Bell was going in right next to her eldest sister and younger brother, though Hunter knew she would much rather have been cremated, her ashes sprinkled out by Rebel Lake where she'd had so much fun as a girl.

But it didn't matter what Clara Bell wanted. All that mattered was what Hunter's father wanted. He and Hunter's mother had arrived just that morning, after making the arrangements long distance for the actual service. They would be leaving immediately after the funeral.

After making a quick stop at the massive headstone that sat a few yards away where Hunter's younger brother had been laid to rest.

Travis had been put in the ground with the same fuss that Clara Bell was receiving, with tons of people and flowers and sobbing regrets. Albeit he'd had a ten-gun salute from the local VFW Hall vets thanking him for his service. While the veterans weren't saluting Clara Bell, they were still out en masse.

Hunter stared at the stream of old men clad in their uniforms, their sparse gray hair slicked back, their looks expectant. No doubt they were counting down the minutes until they reached the First Presbyterian reception hall that had been loaded down with casseroles and hams and pies thanks to the local ladies' auxiliary. They'd provided a feast in honor of Clara. Plenty of good food to soften the blow of everyone's loss.

But there was nothing that could ease the pain twisting inside of Hunter. The anguish because he'd been too late to say good-bye.

Hell, he'd never thought to say any such thing. Clara had always been a permanent fixture in his life and he'd never even considered that there would come a time when she wouldn't be there.

He'd been busy working and doing his best to forget Jenna Tucker.

Going through the motions.

His gaze went to the blonde who stood off to the side with her two sisters and their husbands.

She wore a basic black dress that hit just below the knees. A boxy number that did nothing to accent her curves or show off her luscious tits.

Still his body responded with the same tightening as if she'd been stark naked.

But it wasn't just lust. There was a desperation inside of him that made him want to walk over, slide his arms around her, and never let go.

But he'd already let go. He'd said good-bye. Not officially, mind you. He'd sent her a text that said he was busy. But it was the underlying message that mattered.

It was over.

Done.

"Don't forget to send out the thank-you notes," his father said just to his right. "And make sure you send a personal note to the reverend for all the kind words."

"I'll take care of it, Dad."

"And make sure to send a nice donation to the ladies' auxiliary," his mother reminded him somewhere to his left. "We stopped by the church on the way over and they did a lovely job with the food."

"Consider it done," he said, even though he knew his mother would go ahead and send her own note anyway.

Even after ten years, she still didn't trust him. Not the way she'd trusted Travis.

"Judge Spears tells me you haven't turned in your paperwork for the next election."

"It's done. I just need to drop it off."

"And don't forget—"

"I've got it," Hunter growled, his gaze catching his father's. "I'm a grown-ass man. I can handle myself."

His dad didn't say anything for a long moment. He finally nodded and excused himself to catch up to the reverend. No doubt to issue a verbal thank you because he didn't think his son was capable of doing that either.

"I'm really sorry about Clara." It was the same sentiment, but the voice was different from all the others. Softer. More familiar.

His heart stalled as he turned to see Jenna standing in front of him, so close he could touch her right here and now, in front of God and everyone, if he had a mind to.

He balled his fingers and kept his hands at his side.

"She was really sweet."

"You talked to her," he said. "Pam told me about your visit. Right before she gave me the letters."

"I should have told you—"

"You don't owe me anything. They were her letters, not mine. You did the right thing giving them to her."

"P.J. wasn't the father," she told him. When she noted the surprise in his gaze, she added, "I thought so, too, but when I gave them to Clara she told me it was her Physics teacher."

"Why all the letters to P.J. then?"

"She said he was her best friend. He took the fall for

getting her pregnant and claimed the child as his own because she asked him to. Because she wanted to protect the real father."

And P.J. had done it because he loved her.

"Did she tell you who he was?"

Jenna shook her head, her blonde hair catching rays of sunlight. "I didn't ask. I know he's a Tucker. I've been racking my brain, but the name P.J. just doesn't ring a bell. Does it sound familiar to you?"

Not to Hunter.

Not until he turned and one of the VFW vets caught his eye. He noted the sadness on the man's face, the cluster of gardenias in his hand, and he knew the truth even before he saw the shiny gold name tag that read Purvis Jeremiah Tucker.

"Shorty Tucker," he murmured as he watched the man standing at the grave site, tears in his eyes. He dropped the handful of gardenias on the casket and suddenly Hunter knew that it wasn't the florist sending his great-grandmother leftovers every week. The gardenias had come from Shorty. Every week. Like clockwork. Because he'd loved her.

Because he'd spent the past seventy something years loving a woman who'd never loved him back.

"Listen, I'm sorry about the text," he started. "I've just been really busy—"

"It's fine." She waved him off. "If you hadn't sent the text, I would have. It's over. It's better this way." She glanced behind her at her sisters who'd already started to retreat toward the line of cars. "I should really go. I took so long getting everything out of the house, so they're just now getting to the demolition. Brody is at the house now. I should be there when it starts."

"They're taking down the entire house?"

She nodded.

"And you're really good with that?"

"I am." She seemed to think. "I should be." Then, as if she'd said too much already, she turned. "Take care."

He watched her walk away and barely resisted the urge to grab her hand, haul her close, and just feel her there beside him. To feel just a little less lonely.

But she was right.

It was better for them to be apart.

If only it felt that way.

CHAPTER 31

"And you're good with that?"

Hunter's question followed Jenna home, to the empty house and the massive bulldozer that sat in the front yard.

"She's here," Brody called out to his brother who sat in the dozer seat. "You can rev her up and take her down now."

The engine fired to a blasting rumble, the tires started to roll, and panic welled inside of Jenna because she'd lied to Hunter.

She wasn't good with anything. Not with the demolition of the house, or with the cryptic text message that had informed her that he was calling it quits between them.

She wasn't good.

She was miserable.

As much as she wanted to change her life, she wasn't ready to lose the one place that housed so many memories.

Good and bad.

She'd loved her grandfather and while he might not have returned that love to the extent that she would have liked, he'd still loved her in his own way

She'd seen it when he'd bought her that first ice cream sandwich, she'd felt it every time he'd laughed at something she'd done or called her a chip off the old block.

A bad thing or so she'd always thought. But to him . . . She'd been someone special, just as he was special to her.

She didn't want to forget. To trade the ice cream sandwiches for sorbet for the rest of her life.

"Stop!" she called out. "Please. *Stop*."

The dozer came to a halt just a few inches shy of the front porch as she raced up, waving her arms, desperation bleeding through her. "You can't take down the house."

"Sure we can. I've got the permit right here," Brody said, touching a hand to his pocket. "Or maybe I left it on the desk back at the office. Either way, it's all nice and legal."

"That's not what I'm talking about. I mean, I don't want you to tear it down."

"But it's a mess. It's an electrical nightmare, not to mention the pipes. They're rotting as we speak."

"I know all of that, but surely we can redo all of that without demolishing the entire thing."

Brody seemed to think. "Well, we could do a renovation, but just like I told you before, it'll cost you more than just starting from scratch."

More money for the house meant less money to sink into her business.

Then again, she made a decent salary. If she had to bide her time working a little longer, it would be worth it to save the place. "That's fine. I don't care what it costs. I want to keep the house."

The engine died. Brody smiled.

And it was done.

If only she could hold onto Hunter just as easily.

But he didn't want her and so it didn't matter how she felt.

She was Shorty Tucker and he was the elusive Clara Bell.

And the future looked miserable for them both.

Hunter stood near the corral and watched the next cowboy climb up on top of the bucking bronc. The air horn sounded. The ride lasted all of three seconds because Hell Raiser wasn't about to let anyone get the best of him.

He tossed the cowboy and nearly stomped him into the ground.

"Tricky fucker," the cowboy grumbled as he snatched up his hat and dusted it off as the horse bucked his way toward the opposite end of the corral courtesy of the cowboys maneuvering him into the pen.

"Try not holding on so tight," Hunter called out. "You're making her nervous."

The man's head snapped up, his eyes blazing as they met Hunter's. "If I don't loosen my grip, I won't make it out of the chute."

But he was wrong. Hunter knew it because he'd ridden horses like Hell Raiser before. Sure, he hadn't made it to the professional level, but he'd been on his way.

Before Travis had died.

His brother's image rose up, reminding him of his responsibilities and the all-important fact that he'd been headed to City Hall, not the rodeo arena.

His parents had left right after the funeral and Hunter had made it through just a few minutes of the reception before he'd bailed to get back to work.

To the business of his future.

He turned and crossed the distance back to his SUV. Climbing inside, he stared at the stack of documents sitting on the seat. The check that would pay the filing fee for him to join the ballot in the next election. The application that contained all of his personal information. The required list of constituent signatures to support his run. It was all ready to go.

It was just a matter of dropping everything off.

He keyed the engine and was just about to pull out of the parking lot when Marge's voice came over the radio.

"I've got that address for Boris Miller if you want to pay him a visit. I know it's not a good day for you, but I also know that you like to bury your head in work. So do you want it or what?"

Later. That's what he should have told her.

He glanced at the paperwork again. "Give it to me." He punched the address she read off into his GPS. "Thanks, Marge."

"You bet. And I know you didn't eat a thing after the funeral, so there's a sack lunch in your glove compartment."

"What would I do without you?"

"Get married and settle down. At least that's what I'm hoping."

"What's that supposed to mean?"

"I'm old. Too old to sit behind this desk and listen to my arteries harden for another year. James and me want to travel. This Clara business has us both thinking about how precious time is. So we've decided to pull the trigger and buy that RV we've been pining over for years now. They're running a flash weekend sale down at the dealership and, well, we're not getting any younger."

"Which means you're giving me your two weeks' notice?"

"Actually, it's three. We're springing for a custom outdoor kitchen on our Sandpiper, so they have to special order it from Houston. It'll be here in two and a half weeks. A day or two to pack it up and you're on your own."

"I hate to lose you."

"Yeah, yeah. Well, just remember that you've got to eat. And it might be nice to do that with a member of the opposite sex, hence the hint about settling down and finding a wife."

"Message received."

"Speaking of messages. Bobby's looking for you. Something about you playing bunko tonight with him and his wife and her cousin. He said you promised."

"Bunko? Tonight?"

"It might be a good time to start looking for that wife."

"I hate bunko."

"Yeah, well sometimes we make concessions for those we love. You watch your six," she murmured and the mic went silent.

Bunko? With Kaitlyn?

It would be a good time to get to know her.

On the other hand, the thought of sitting with anyone other than Jenna bothered him a hell of a lot more than it should have.

Especially since Jenna wasn't his woman.

He told himself that, but deep in his gut he couldn't forget the feel of her hands on his body, her taste on his lips, her voice in his head.

He would find a wife someday.

In the future.

But damned if he didn't find himself thinking about it today. About Jenna and how it just might be nice to wake up to her every morning.

He punched the address Marge texted him into his GPS and followed the instructions to Farm Road 52. He hung a left and ate up pavement, heading for the small house tucked away at the very end of the dirt road, just past a row of run-down trailers.

With a sagging porch and peeling paint, the house wasn't much better than the dilapidated trailers. It was the truck, not the house that made him think that maybe, just maybe he might have hit pay dirt.

A brand new 4 x 4 Ford Dually sat in the drive. Shiny black. Expensive.

Too much so for a poor farmer with a falling-down house.

But a moonshiner with a top-notch setup?

Hunter killed the engine, checked his gun, and climbed out.

There was only one way to find out.

CHAPTER 32

It was Boris Miller.

Hunter knew it even before he found himself staring down the barrel of a sawed-off shotgun.

His gut told him as much before Boris opened the door and met him with the gun. That, and Hunter saw what was left of the game camera sitting on a small table on the front porch, next to a jar of crystal-clear moonshine.

"I was wondering when you might come calling, Sheriff."

"That's quite a setup you've got for yourself."

"You saw that, huh?" He shook his head. "I was afraid of that when I heard what happened with the Mayweathers. They tried to tell me it was a hog, but I know better. Ain't no hog can hop around on two legs."

"Hiring them was your first mistake."

"Actually, that was just another in a long line of mistakes. It seems it's not as easy to set up shop the way it used to be, what with the Feds looking over your shoulder and the local police busting your chops. When my granddaddy used to cook, it was a more simple time. If a man had a good recipe, then he didn't need to worry about all the piddly details. Folks liked his product, then everything else just fell in line. The cops looked the other way and no one was the wiser."

"I don't look the other way."

"That's why it has to come to this"—he pointed the gun at Hunter's chest—"this is going to clean up all of my mess."

"What do you mean?"

"I'm going to take you out, Sheriff DeMassi. Once and for all. You're too nosey for one thing." His grin faltered. "And much too smart. Then again, if you were that smart, you would've stopped sniffing around after James Harlin bit the dust. So maybe you aren't all that, after all."

"What's that supposed to mean?"

But Hunter knew even before the man opened his mouth. Boris was the one responsible for the explosion that killed Jenna's grandfather. While some other local moonshiners had been suspect, Hunter had never been able to pin it on any one. Not only was the evidence circumstantial, but he'd just had this gut feeling that there was more.

That something bigger had happened than a freak accident caused by a careless cook.

"Tell me what happened to James Harlin."

Boris's expression drew into a tight frown. "We've talked enough. Why don't you start walking." He nudged Hunter's chest with the rifle. "Head around back and don't stop until I tell you."

"Sure thing." His steps were careful. Paced. "Tell me about Tucker," he said again.

"Why should I?" The barrel jabbed between his

shoulder blades as Boris came up behind him, following him around the house. "You're the law. You should have figured it out for yourself by now. Hell, I figured you had all the answers when you started staking out my still. You see, there's only so much room for moonshine in this county. I'm a simple man. I ain't into hauling my supply across state lines like some. I'd rather make my money right here. But I couldn't very well do that with James Harlin peddling his. Him and Big Jimmy Ham were both running some decent stills and cutting into my profit margin. I had to take them both out. I took care of James Harlin first."

The pieces started to fall into place then. James Harlin had been too experienced to blow himself up. That, and there had been clues. The unusual footprint at the explosion site. The clues inside the house that said James wasn't the pickled drunk that so many thought.

Hunter had gone through the man's room and found so many pictures of his granddaughters. Drawings they'd done for him. Even a few baby teeth stuffed into a small box in his sock drawer. They'd been hidden away. The man hadn't been the type to wear his emotions on his sleeve. But he'd had them. He'd felt them. He'd loved his granddaughters as much as he'd been able to.

Too much to blow himself up.

"I was going after Big Jimmy and his boys," Boris went on, "when you started poking around. You busted them and took them out of the picture for me, which is why I'm going to make this quick and painless for you. You saved me a lot of trouble. It's only right I give tit-for-tat. I'm a reasonable man, after all"

"You can't just think you can shoot me and get away with it."

"Actually, I'm not going to shoot you at all." He urged Hunter around to the small shed that sat in the far rear of the backyard several yards from the run-down house. "I'm going to let my dogs take care of you. Pit bulls," Boris added. "See, you came poking around, thinking I was someone of interest. I wasn't here so you kept poking around and stuck your nose where it didn't belong. My dogs got ahold of you 'cause that's what they do— they protect my property from intruders, and that's that. You're gone. The coast is clear. The business keeps running."

"That's crazy."

But it would work. Hunter knew that the minute he heard the growling inside the shed. The dogs were ready to eat anyone alive on command and it was just a matter of time before Boris set them free.

"Hold it right there." He jabbed Hunter again, bringing him to a dead stop. "Down on your knees."

Hunter didn't move for a long second until the rifle pressed into the back of his head. "Down or I'll shoot you where you stand and then let the dogs have what's left. No medical examiner will be able to make heads or tails of you after that."

Hunter hit the dirt and watched as Boris came around him, the gun still pointed at Hunter's head. The man backed up to the shed. A smile and the man brought the gun up and bashed the lock in with the butt of his gun as if Hunter had been looking around and tried to get in himself.

Just like that, the door opened.

Boris whistled and the dogs sprang into action.

Hunter went for his gun, but he was too late. Teeth closed around his wrist and he fell backward.

The next few seconds passed in a rush of white-hot pain and dripping blood, followed by several loud gunshots.

When Hunter managed to open his eyes, he saw Boris standing above him, a crazed look on his face as he stared past Hunter to some unknown point behind.

"You killed my dogs, you sonofabitch!" he wailed.

He raised the rifle and took aim. A shot rang out and Hunter waited to feel the bullet rip into his flesh.

Instead, he watched as Boris stumbled backward. Dirt sprayed as deadweight hit the ground with a thud, a bright red stain spreading across the man's T-shirt.

"Sheriff?" Bobby's voice rang out. "Are you okay?"

Hunter got to his feet, gun in hand as he nudged Boris to make sure the man was down for good. "I'm fine."

"You don't look fine. You look like chewed-up kibble. At least your arm does."

"Thanks a lot."

"We'd better call an ambulance."

"That would be a good idea," Hunter said, his vision starting to blur. He was dripping an awful lot of blood.

"I guess that means you won't be able to double-date tonight?" Bobby went on as if they were just wrapping up any given day at the office. "Kaitlyn was really hoping . . ."

"Can't," Hunter managed before the darkness overtook him. "I'm already seeing someone."

"Really?"

"Really." And then he closed his eyes and let the blackness overwhelm him.

"It's about time you woke up." Jenna's familiar voice pushed through the nothingness that engulfed Hunter and drew him back to the hospital room and the woman sitting beside his bed. "I stopped by the station and Marge told me what happened. I'm glad you're okay."

"A little chewed up, but I'll make it." He ignored the crazy stutter of his heart because she was here, now, and suddenly there was too much to say and not enough words. He swallowed against the burning in his throat and fought to find them anyway. "I need to tell you something."

"Bobby already did. He said Boris confessed that he killed my granddad."

He nodded. "He wanted him out of the way so that he was the only one making moonshine in this county."

"But James Harlin barely made enough to get him into a Friday night card game down at the VFW Hall. He couldn't have been much of a threat."

"It doesn't matter. He was still competition." He noted the brightness of her eyes and added, "I'm really sorry."

"Thanks." She sniffled. "And thanks for not giving up on the truth. I know you kept looking into it when you didn't have to. Everyone else wanted to write it off as an accident."

"I needed to know."

The digging deep, the figuring things out, the *knowing* brought the same rush of excitement that he'd felt all those years ago when he'd climbed onto a bucking bronc. That's why he'd buried himself in his work for so long. Because it satisfied the rush.

Almost.

"How's the reconstruction?" he managed.

"You mean remodel." Her smile was small but genuine and he felt the weight on his chest lift a little "I didn't tear down the house."

"That's a good thing."

"It is. I love that house. I know it's a crappy thing to love, but I do."

"That's good."

"Anyhow, I just wanted to make sure you were okay and say thanks for everything you've done."

"Just doing my job."

Disappointment twisted her face for a long moment, as if she'd wanted him to say something else. But then she shrugged. "I guess so."

"How's my favorite patient today?" Marge's voice disrupted the awkward silence that settled between them as the older woman waltzed in with a bouquet of balloons and three women he didn't recognize.

"Oh, hey, Jenna," said one of the women.

"Hi, Ruth Ann."

"I hope I'm not interrupting. I just thought you could use a little company," Marge told Hunter. "This is Carol Foster, Ruth Ann Tucker, and Darla Stanford. They work down at the RV dealership. Ruth Ann's dad is the owner. They're just dying to meet the man who took down the most ruthless moonshiner in this town's history."

"I don't know about ruthless," Hunter started, his gaze fixed on Jenna who inched backward as if trying to shrink away from the crowd. She gave him a little wave and then she turned.

He opened his mouth to stop her, to say something—anything—but then Ruth Ann closed in and the moment was lost.

"Boris was a brutal man," she said. "I'd love to hear how you took him down."

"So would I."

"Me, too."

"I'll just set these here"—Marge placed the teddy bear attached to the balloons on Hunter's tray table—"and give you four some time to yourselves. Don't go getting engaged before I get back now," she murmured with a wink and Hunter knew she'd decided not to let her last three weeks pass idly by. She was going to find him a wife on her own.

And these were the first three candidates.

If only he'd wanted any of them half as much as he wanted Jenna Tucker.

CHAPTER 33

Kim Bowman damned herself a thousand times.

It was just supposed to be dinner. They'd both been picking through the food choices at the reception following Clara Bell Sawyer's funeral, and there'd been nothing that didn't involve cheese or bread crumbs or cream of mushroom soup.

She'd needed a healthy dinner.

Dinner, not dessert.

But she'd been trying to avoid the whole chemistry connection for so long that she'd forgotten how powerful it could be. How one thing could lead to another.

How a simple dinner could go straight to a rich, decadent dessert.

Boy, had she ever.

She closed her eyes, relishing the strong, callused hands that slid over her, tugging at her buttons, pushing at her undies, scraping across her flesh.

Goose bumps danced over her skin and she shivered despite the warm night air.

"Hold up," Carter Walls said, pulling away. "We're both wearing way too many clothes."

He fixed the situation in less than a minute, tugging off his shirt, pitching his jeans and boxer briefs.

She didn't mean to look. She wanted to refuse to give herself a moment to regret or lose her nerve, but she couldn't help herself.

Her gaze drank him in, his broad chest and flat brown nipples surrounded by dark hair. His legs were long and thick with muscles. His arousal was huge and hard, and her heart paused for a long breathless moment.

If she'd thought for even five seconds that he was more of an intellectual with his IT background, she'd been wrong. This guy was pure cowboy, from his ripped biceps to the hard planes of his abdomen, to his corded thighs.

But then the looking was over and the speed picked up again. He reached for her. Flesh met hot flesh and she stopped thinking altogether.

She felt the moist heat of his breath on her breast and then his lips closed over her nipple.

He licked and suckled and nibbled. Sensation skittered along her nerve endings and she forgot all about wanting to feel his lips on her own. Heat pooled low in her belly, making her thighs tremble and her hands quiver. Then his mouth opened and he drew her deeper, sucking hard. Sensation flooded through her, crashing over her in huge waves.

Hands skimmed down her back, around her waist, her rib cage. He moved lower until strong fingers slid between her legs, into her slick flesh. He stroked and coaxed until a shameless moan burst from her lips.

He touched her just so and desire pounded through her as fiercely as a summer storm. Fierce and drenching all at once, yet oddly rejuvenating.

When he slipped a finger into her and pushed deep, she cried out. Her trembling turned to shaking as her entire body reacted to the invasion, her nerves humming from the incredible need swamping her senses.

Her hands stroked up and down his back, grasping his hard, muscled buttocks before she circled his hips. She'd barely brushed his erection when she found her wrist caught in a tight grip . . .

"No," he groaned. "It's been too long and there's no way this is going to go slow if you touch me."

Too long?

No, she was the one who'd gone too long. She didn't do this kind of thing. She was into nice, not wild and wicked and dangerous.

But she felt all three at the moment, and suddenly she couldn't help herself. "Do it," she begged. "Do it right now." The desperation in her voice surprised her, but she was beyond caring. She trembled and throbbed and ached so badly. "Please."

He scooped her into his arms and headed for her bedroom. The mattress met her back and then he disappeared. A few minutes later, he reappeared, condom in hand and slid the latex down his engorged length. He covered her then, spreading her legs wide and positioning himself.

The voluptuous head of his hot erection nudged her slick opening and every nerve in her body jumped to full alert. His chest heaved, crushing her tender breasts as he fought to drag air into his lungs.

"Christ, I don't know what it is about you," he murmured, staring at her as if she were some impossible puzzle he just couldn't begin to solve, and then the contemplation ended. He thrust into her, stretching and filling and, *ahhh* . . .

"Wrap your legs around me," he murmured, and she quickly complied, the motion drawing him deeper. So deliciously deep.

Carter reached under her and clasped her hips, angling her as he withdrew and thrust into her again. And again.

This was it.

She'd meant to lay back and enjoy every touch, every sound, to commit it to memory for all the so-so encounters with Gabe or Benny or whoever she ended up with.

She couldn't.

Despite the intense pleasure he was giving her, she suddenly wanted more. She wanted him harder and deeper and faster and she couldn't help herself. She clutched his slick shoulders, his back, his buttocks, lifted her pelvis and matched his rhythm. Her nipples rubbed against the soft hair on his chest, sending ripples of heat through her body. The pressure built as he pumped into her, pushing her higher. Like a fierce lightning flash, the pressure hit. Her back arched and she shattered. Wave after wave of luscious heat rolled over her, through her. Her muscles contracted, gripping him tight and wringing a deep groan from him.

He quickly followed her over the edge, his muscles as hard as granite as he plunged into her one last, sweet time. He collapsed on top of her, his chest heaving, his heart thundering in sync with her own.

He slid his strong arms around her, rolled over, and gathered her close, and contentment unlike anything she'd ever felt before rushed through her. She snuggled deeper into Carter's embrace and closed her eyes.

And then she cursed the Powers That Be for sending her the wrong man. And for making him feel so right.

CHAPTER 34

"This is it," Jenna told Callie and Brandy as she set the box on one of the tables at Sweet Somethings. The bakery had closed up shop over an hour ago and the place sat empty. "Everything James Harlin kept hidden away at the house."

Hidden because their granddad hadn't been a man to show his feelings. He hadn't liked feeling, period. Not since he'd lost his precious wife all those years ago.

He'd hurt so bad after the loss that he'd retreated into a bottle and while Jenna had been too young to understand what he'd been thinking at the time, it was more than evident now.

James Harlin Tucker had been determined to numb himself. To keep from feeling ever again so that he didn't have to go through the same pain that had nearly destroyed him when he'd buried his beloved.

And so he'd kept his distance from any and everyone after that, particularly the three little girls who'd invaded his home, and his heart.

She knew that now after uncovering all of the small things hidden away in the back of his dresser drawers and the empty spaces under his bed and the deep recesses of his closet.

And it was high time her sisters knew as well.

She watched as Callie reached into the box and retrieved a faded drawing that sat on top. "I did this at Vacation Bible school back when I was eight." She eyed the red crayon depiction of their house, along with the barn out back and the old man sitting in his rocker on the front porch. "I thought he threw this away."

"He didn't throw anything away," Jenna told them. She grabbed a small baggie filled with some dried up wildflowers that had long since withered and faded, and handed them to a stunned Brandy. "You gave these to him on his birthday. You remember that?"

The shock turned to soft wonder as her sister's eyes brightened. "I don't understand."

"He wasn't a jackass because he couldn't help it. He was a jackass because it was easier. He didn't want to feel anything for us."

"But he did," Jenna pointed out. "That's why he kept all of this stuff. Because it meant something. He just didn't want to admit it. To *feel* it."

"To hurt," Callie added. "Mama used to tell me how much he cried at grandma's funeral. I never believed her. He was always so cold and stoic, except when he was drinking. And then he was just a downright jerk."

"Being a jerk kept us at arm's length," Jenna said. "It wasn't the right thing to do, but that's what he did. The important thing is that we know he loved us."

Brandy reached into the box and retrieved another drawing. This one depicting a birthday cake she'd done for him ages ago. "He did. In his own way, he did."

"It doesn't matter," Callie said. "It doesn't change what an asshole he was."

But it did.

Jenna could see it in the softness of her eldest sister's eyes, the small smile that played on her lips when she retrieved a tiny braided key chain she'd made as a Christmas present for him back when she'd been in the second grade.

It changed things for Callie, all right. And Brandy, as well, who sniffled as she stared at the stack of recipe cards she'd given him for yet a different birthday with all of his favorite foods written in green crayon and the promise to one day make each and every one for him.

"I never thought he cared about any of this."

"He did. James Harlin cared about us," Jenna said, retrieving the miniature American Girl doll from one of the McDonald's Happy Meals he'd bought for her. "He loved us."

And for the first time, the three Tucker sisters actually believed it.

He wasn't going after her.

Hunter steeled himself against the nearly overwhelming urge and watched as she disappeared inside the motel room. While Jenna had decided not to demolish the house, she'd still had to move out for the reconstruction.

She'd moved in right next door to the Dairy Freeze, directly across the street from the station and so he'd seen her each and every day since he'd returned to work last week after being released from the hospital.

The longest week of his life as he'd wrestled with his

feelings and the truth—that he wasn't ready to say good-bye to Jenna Tucker. Not now.

Not ever.

He'd finally decided to stop with all the pleasantries and tell her that he still wanted her. That he didn't want to want her, but he did, and there it was.

She hadn't been nearly as receptive as he'd hoped.

"Are you kidding me?" she'd demanded. "You want to pick up where we left off?"

He'd meant it to sound much more romantic, but when she'd repeated his words back to him, he'd realized how fucked up it had all sounded.

That's not the only thing he wanted.

The door shut and the lights flicked on inside and still, he didn't move.

It's over, buddy. She said so. You said so. Get over it.

He wanted to.

He wanted to turn and walk away the way he would have with any other woman.

But this was Jenna.

She was different. Special.

The truth rumbled from down deep, stirring a rush of denial as fierce as the emotion himself. Special? Hell, no. She was no such thing. She was like any other woman and no way did he actually love her.

Love wasn't in the cards for them any more than it had been for Clara Bell and Shorty.

Shorty had been a sucker. Loving a woman who'd loved another. Loving her for so many years even though she didn't love him back.

As much as he wanted to condemn Shorty for being so foolish, he couldn't.

Because he knew how the old man felt. He knew what it was like to want to make someone else happy.

He fought the truth and turned on his heel. He didn't love her and she didn't love him, and that was good.

Easier.

He held tight to the thought, climbed into his SUV, and headed back to work.

If only he could shake the feeling that he was about to make the biggest mistake of his life.

CHAPTER 35

Jenna had spent the night tossing and turning and replaying her last conversation with Hunter. And wishing with all of her heart that it had gone differently.

That he hadn't asked to pick up where they'd left off because she didn't just want to fall back into bed with him.

She wanted more.

Everything.

A truth that haunted her as she made her way out to watch Brody and his brothers start on the renovation to the kitchen. They'd finished the electrical and the plumbing and were starting room by room with the upgrades. Today was the new cabinet installation and she wanted to see how the dark cherry looked against the new countertops. It looked great, but the site didn't fill her with even the slightest excitement. Not with Hunter still heavy on her mind and her feelings for him swimming down deep.

She'd wanted so desperately to take him up on his offer, to pick up where they'd left off with the physical and feel him at least one more time.

She didn't just want sex.

But he did.

He'd never said one word otherwise.

Instead, he'd simply stood there in front of her motel room long after she'd gone inside.

While she might have fallen in love with him, he wasn't in love with her.

Which was fine.

Really.

She didn't need Hunter DeMassi anyway. She had her house and her property. Plenty of room to build an extra structure and start her own equine center.

In due time.

Her money was invested in the renovation right now, but it was just a matter of keeping her nose to the grindstone. She had to keep going. Fighting.

As for Hunter . . .

He was back at work, back doing a job that kept him going but didn't feed the passion inside of him. He loved horses, too, he just wouldn't let himself give in to the emotion. Act on it.

Not with the wild broncs, and not with her. He was stuck, just as Clara had been, and like his great-grandmother, he was going to stick it out. To endure instead of living.

Jenna wasn't falling into the same trap. She was living for herself. Really and truly *living*.

If she didn't drop dead of a heart attack first.

She clutched her chest and stared at the familiar man standing in her front yard.

"Chuck?" She eyed the black leather pants and sleeveless vest. "What are you wearing?"

"You said you wanted something different, Jenna. Something more bad ass. Well, here I am."

"I didn't mean I wanted *you* to be different," she started, but he held up a hand.

"I know what you want. You want a man to take charge." He crossed the distance to her. "Well, that's what I'm doing." And then he ducked, his shoulder catching her in the middle as he tossed her over his shoulder.

"Let me down right now." She pounded his back, but it only seemed to make him that much more determined. "I mean it, Chuck. This is crazy."

"Crazy wild," he said as he strode toward a black Jeep with temporary tags. "The rental car place didn't have a motorcycle, so I had to settle for this. But I've applied for a loan with my credit union. As soon as I get the approval, I'm heading to Austin and the nearest Harley dealership."

"Go wherever you want, but put me down first."

"Sorry, but us strong, alpha males take charge."

"I mean it. Put me down right now or you'll be sorry."

"No can do."

"I mean it . . ." she started, pounding harder, but the deep voice drowned her out.

"You heard the lady. Put her down." Hunter's deep voice echoed in her ears and she twisted, catching a glimpse of his uniform-clad body just a few feet away.

"Of course, Sheriff." Chuck let go and she slid to the ground like a sack. "We were just role playing. You know how couples do."

"Is that what you're doing?"

"Exactly. See, Jenna, here, likes a more take-charge kind of guy so I ordered a few things on Leatherup.com and here I am."

"How do you know what Jenna likes?" Jealousy

burned hot and bright in his gaze and a strange sense of hope spread through Jenna. As if he really and truly did love her.

But then that wasn't the problem. It was him admitting his feelings. Acting on them.

"I do like a more take-charge kind of guy," Jenna cut in, climbing to her feet. "I like a man who isn't afraid to be himself."

"But I did that," Chuck started.

"Not you," she told the man before turning to Hunter. "I'm talking to you." She planted her hands on her hips and eyed him. "You're afraid."

The declaration made his frown that much deeper and unease zapped her. But she'd already opened her mouth and the real Jenna, the one she'd been trying to change for the past few months, wasn't about to shut up.

"You're afraid to love me. To love anything. Because you're afraid if you do, then no one will love you."

"You talk too much, you know that?"

"Guilty as charged, Sheriff. But that still doesn't change anything. You're afraid, but you don't have to be."

"Really? And why is that?"

"Because I love you anyway."

He didn't say anything for a long moment. Instead, he simply stared at her before he finally opened his mouth and murmured, "It's not about being afraid. It's about keeping a promise." He turned then and walked away.

And she knew this time he wasn't coming back.

He was nipping this in the bud right now.

That's what Hunter told himself as he headed to City

Hall to file his papers for the next election. He'd made his choices and while he wasn't all that happy with them at the moment, a man *had* to keep his word and do the right thing.

That's what Hunter told himself, he just wasn't so sure he believed it anymore. Because he'd changed.

He didn't feel so indifferent inside. So contained. So suppressed.

He *felt*, period. And that was good. Useless, but good.

Hunter pulled into the parking lot and walked into the lobby.

The soft voice sounded directly behind him and he turned to see Jenna standing in the doorway.

She wore a Giddy Up T-shirt tucked into a fitted black miniskirt that hugged her in all the right places. But it wasn't the outfit that stalled the air in his lungs. It was the gleam in her eyes.

"I told you this isn't going to work," he managed, despite a suddenly dry throat.

"I know what you said, but you're full of shit. It can work. That's what really scares you. Not the notion of failing, but that you might be happy. Too happy, and you don't think you deserve to be happy because your brother's the one who deserves to be here. Not you. That's what you really think, isn't it? What eats at you. Why him and not you?"

"It should have been me," he said, the feelings pushing and pulling and finally boiling over so fiercely that he couldn't keep the lid on them a moment more. "I was always pushing the limits, climbing on the back of a bronc, living like there was no tomorrow. I was only thinking about myself, but my brother spent his life thinking about other people. That's admirable. That's deserving. He deserved to live, not me."

"That's not your call, don't you know that? That's life, and death. We don't get to pick the latter, but we can damn sure make the most of the former. We have to deal with what we're dealt. He's not here for whatever reason, but you are and you can't keep punishing yourself because of that. You're here, Hunter, and that's okay."

It was.

Hunter realized that as he saw her staring up at him, her eyes full of gratitude because unlike his folks who couldn't see past their own pain, she could and she saw him. The real man. The good. And the bad.

And she loved him anyway.

"It doesn't change anything," he told her.

"Because you don't love me," she stated. "That's it, isn't it? I convinced myself on the drive over here that you didn't say the words because maybe, just maybe you were as scared as I was, but that's not it, is it? You don't feel the same."

"No, I meant that I already filed my paperwork. I'm on the ticket."

"Oh." The truth seemed to hit her and a grin curved her beautiful lips. "Well, then, I guess we'll have to see what we can do about losing this election, Sheriff."

"What's that supposed to mean?"

"Well, you're going to be much too busy helping with my horses and teaching down at the rodeo arena to have any time left over for law and order. That means we'll have to do whatever's necessary to make sure you're not expected to keep the peace." She stepped up to him then, her hand going to his chest. "I think a little lewd and lascivious behavior smack-dab in front of the courthouse is a good start, don't you?"

And then she kissed him with a fierceness that had people gasping and gossiping.

Unease rushed through him, followed by a sense of joy so profound that he knew he could never turn and walk away from her. Not now. Not twenty years from now. Not ever.

What's more, he didn't want to walk away.

It was time to stop pretending. Time to love someone. To trust someone enough to let them love him.

A strange sense of peace stole through him, and for the first time in a long time, he didn't give a lick who was watching him or what they thought.

"I do love you." He said the words he'd felt for so long but had refused to admit. "More than anything."

Her panic faded into a look of pure delight as she broke the kiss and pulled away. "Does that mean you're up to joining forces and raising some horses together?"

He grinned and tightened his hold on her. "'Til death do us part, baby. 'Til death do us part."

"That sounds like a proposal more than a job offer."

His grin faded as he stared deep into her eyes. "Will you marry me, Jenna, and make me the happiest man alive?"

"I will," she murmured. "I do." And then she kissed him and left no doubt in his mind that she meant every word.

EPILOGUE

"I must be seeing things." Hunter DeMassi's voice carried across the flower-filled courtyard that sat between the Rebel First Presbyterian Church and the massive reception hall behind it. "I can't believe it. You came."

Gator Hallsey closed the few yards that separated them, his polished black cowboy boots clattering on the stone walkway. "I said I would, didn't I?" And Gator always kept his word.

At least where Hunter was concerned.

It didn't matter that he hadn't been inside of a church since his grandmother, God rest her soul, had toted him to Sunday school when he'd been barely knee-high. Or that he was about to stand up in front of a roomful of people that included the entire Rebel County Sheriff's office and several bigwigs from Austin. Feds even, judging by the cluster of black SUVs situated in the parking lot.

He ignored the sense of unease that rolled through him and gave Hunter a wink. "I can't let you get hitched without a Best Man, now can I?"

"Thanks, man." Hunter clapped him on the shoulder just as a middle-aged woman rushed up, a single red rose in one hand and a lethal-looking stickpin in the other.

"Is this him?" Mabel Leroy Tucker asked.

"The one and only." Hunter grinned.

"We thought you weren't coming." Mabel grimaced as she stepped up in front of Gator. "I specifically told everyone in the bridal party to be here a half hour early."

"Gator's here against his will," Hunter offered. "He's not a big believer when it comes to matrimony."

"Nonsense," Mabel muttered. "Matrimony is the most wonderful thing in the world." She grasped the black satin lapel of the tuxedo coat that he wore with a pair of starched Wranglers and a stiff white dress shirt.

He ignored the urge to tug at the collar.

At least Hunter hadn't forced him into a complete monkey suit. He and Jenna had wanted a country wedding and so they'd let the groomsmen keep their jeans and boots and, as far as Gator was concerned, their dignity.

As much as any man could muster with the bridal march blaring in his ears.

"Hold still," she murmured, coming at him with the pearl-tipped straight pin. "There." She smoothed his jacket and straightened his collar for a split second before responding to something someone said over the Bluetooth hooked over her ear. "No, no," she shrieked, nearly splintering his eardrum. "The rose petals are for the flower girl. Do *not* sprinkle them on the cake table. They'll clash with the sugar flowers on the cake . . ." Her voice trailed off as she shook her head and turned on her heel. "No, no, *no*. Don't give her the flower basket yet. She's only three years old. They'll be all over the ground before the processional even starts. Or worse. Remember the flower girl at the Canyon-Guthrie wedding? She ate them like popcorn. We had to take her to the ER to get her stomach pumped smack-dab in the middle of the reception. Just hold onto it. I'm coming. I'll get her situated in the wagon and then we'll hand her the basket. Five minutes," she called over her shoulder to Hunter and Gator. "The reverend will signal when it's time." And then she disappeared through the side door that led into the main sanctuary.

"You sure about this?" Gator asked, stepping up to his old friend.

He and Hunter had been inseparable back in the day, before Hunter's brother had died and he'd traded in his wicked ways in favor of civic duty.

"Are you kidding? I've never been more sure of anything in my life." He turned and stared through the side window of the church, at the bridal party milling about in the foyer.

His attention fixed solely on the woman in white. Jenna Tucker did make one hell of a vision in a fitted white dress. One that quickly ducked back behind a massive fern when she caught Gator looking in at her.

"You know it's my duty as your best man to make sure you realize what you're getting into."

"Actually, it's your duty to get me to the altar no matter what."

"Maybe. But it's my duty as your friend to lead the way should you want to make a fast getaway. This is the real deal, man. No going back." Gator's gaze went to Callie Tucker Sawyer, the matron of honor, who wore a fitted red dress that matched the red rose bouquet in her hand and accented the baby growing inside of her. She was due any time now by the looks of her and thrilled to death if the smile on her face was any indication. She held tight to her husband, Brett, who wore the same get-up as Gator. Next to them stood Brandy Tucker Mc-Call, matron of honor number two, and her groomsman husband, Tyler.

Both men had sown their own wild oats back in the day and so Gator had crossed paths with them many times over the years.

But not lately.

They'd settled down with the Tucker sisters and while Gator, himself, would sooner kick his own ass than waltz down the aisle, he had to admit that both men looked extremely happy.

As happy as the groom.

Yeah, right.

Their cat's-got-the-canary expressions were no doubt due to the mason jars filled with Texas Thunder Tea, a blend of the infamous Sawyer-Tucker moonshine now being distributed by Foggy Bottom Distillers and Miss Mabel's sweet Texas tea. The ribbon-wrapped jars were being handed out as a signature cocktail to the guests who mingled in the nearby garden area before heading inside for the ceremony. No doubt both men had downed a few pints in preparation for the hot-as-hell tuxedo jackets.

Gator wished he'd arrived a few minutes sooner and grabbed a jar of his own. Maybe then he wouldn't be so antsy, as if he were the one about to hang up his precious bachelor card. But then he'd been hard-pressed to get here in the nick of time after this last run from Houston.

He'd delivered a trunkful of premium hooch to a golf pro who lived in River Oaks. A man who could have easily bought his liquor through the proper channels.

But that wasn't nearly as much fun.

There was something taboo about hooking up with a bootlegger and buying a jug of pure liquid fire. Or so Jeff Something-or-other had told him when he'd made his delivery.

It was all about the novelty of it.

Luckily there were plenty still fascinated with the old school art of shine to keep Gator and his two partners hauling butt six days out of seven.

"You ought to think about slowing down yourself," Hunter told him, as if noting the exhaustion tugging at his muscles.

He grinned. "Plenty of time for that when I'm six feet under. Besides, with you stepping down as sheriff to help Jenna with her horses, I was actually thinking about expanding my business." He winked. "No more conflict of interest."

Hunter grinned. "I wouldn't do that if I were you. Bobby isn't likely to look the other way now that he's wearing the badge."

"Bobby's not nearly fast enough to catch me and you damn well know it."

"Maybe not now, but everybody has to slow down eventually." Hunter's eyes gleamed. "Settle down. Even the infamous Gator Hallsey."

Gator wasn't sure why the words suddenly bothered him. Sure, at thirty-four he was getting older. But he was still as fast as he'd ever been. Faster even.

As for settling down . . .

He'd yet to meet a woman hot enough, sweet enough, to make him want to hang up his hat and kick off his boots for anything longer than a one-night stand.

"You might be snapping on the old ball and chain, but don't try to take me down with you. I like being single."

"That's what I used to say, but then I met Jenna. Speaking of meeting someone, Bobby's got this friend. Her name's Kaitlyn," Hunter started, but then the side door opened and Thomas Rhett's "Die a Happy Man" drifted from inside.

"It's time," said the reverend who ducked out and motioned to Hunter.

Thankfully.

Because the last thing Gator wanted was to hear Hunter DeMassi, his old running buddy, suggest a fix-up.

Gator Hallsey liked being single. Hell, he loved it.

Then again, his buddy sure as hell did look happy.

The notion struck and instead of grabbing Hunter's arm and hauling him the other way, he clapped him on the back and smiled. "Let's go get you married, buddy."

Don't miss more Rebel Moonshine novels by
Kimberly Raye

TEXAS THUNDER
RED-HOT TEXAS NIGHTS

Available from St. Martin's Paperbacks